I Can't Tell You

Other Graphia Titles

Story for a Black Night
by Clayton Bess

Comfort
by Carolee Dean

3 NBs of Julian Drew
by James M. Deem

48 Shades of Brown
by Nick Earls

Not As Crazy As I Seem
by George Harrar

Owl in Love
by Patrice Kindl

Zazoo
by Richard Mosher

The Road to Damietta
by Scott O'Dell

I Can't Tell You

hillary frank

AN IMPRINT OF HOUGHTON MIFFLIN COMPANY
BOSTON

www.houghtonmifflinbooks.com

The text of this book is set in far more typefaces than we'd like + far fewer than you'd think.

Library of Congress Cataloging-in-Publication Data
Frank, Hillary.
I can't tell you / Hillary Frank.
p. cm.
Summary: When Jake says something he regrets during a fight over a girl with his best friend and college roommate, he begins communicating only through notes and letters, but when he wants to tell the girl how he really feels about her, his silence and penchant for puns get in the way.
Paperback ISBN 0-618-49491-X
[1. Interpersonal relations—Fiction. 2. Mutism, Elective—Fiction. 3. Letters—Fiction. 4. Puns and punning—Fiction. 5. Colleges and universities—Fiction. 6. Family problems—Fiction.]
I. Title: I can't tell you. II. Title.
PZ7.F8493Iae 2004 [Fic]—dc22 2004007071

Design and composition by Mad Jones Art & Design

Manufactured in the United States of America
HAD 10 9 8 7 6 5

for Josh

A clear crisp night in early November.

Yellow Legal Paper, Folded in Eighths and Stuffed into Jake's Drool-Stained Pillowcase 3:12 a.m.

Xandra,

I think you're faking it. Your eyes are closed, but your breathing—it's not deep enough.

That's OK. I can't relax either.

I'm sorry you had to see me + Sean like that—all pissed and shouty. And that I'm not saying what it's about. I'm also sorry that I said he'd probably come back tonight. Because I'm sure he won't. He's probably staying with his Alpha Pitchfork "brothers." This is the worst we've ever fought. And the truth is ~~See, I pretended like I thought he'd come back because~~ It's just, I thought it would be nice to have you in here. You + me. Alone. Don't worry. I'm not gonna get all freaky on you. Try to coax you out of Sean's bed + into mine.

But g.o.d.d.a.m.n.

I'm tempted as hell to go over there + I don't know... touch your cheeks.

Hey, sicko! You know I meant the ones on your face. Even though Sean would think I mean the ones down below.

Fine, I'll come clean. That's how the fight started. With him thinking I touched your butt when me + you were wrestling over your keys in the leaves. But I didn't touch you there. Did I? Does it matter, anyway? You two aren't even a couple.

And the rest of it. Why we were fighting, I mean. Well, you don't need to know that. Except I'm sure you'll have questions. Because you'll see that Sean won't want to talk to me. And. I'm not sure I can even face him now. After everything I told him. I know. I'm being vague. But it's bad enough that I spilled my guts to Sean. Um, yes, it was messy...

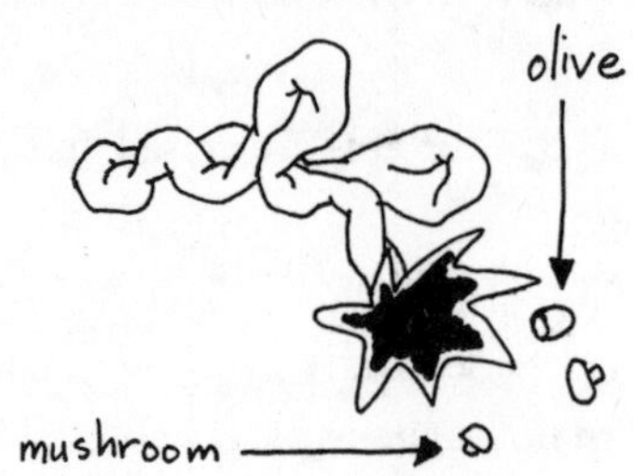

U.g.h. I know it SOUNDS like I'm being the same old me. All jokey + everything. But I don't FEEL like me. After blurting all that stuff out to Sean. You know how people pretend to zip their mouths shut, then lock them + throw away the key? That's what I'd like to do. Minus the pretending part.

But rolling around in the leaves with you. Maybe that was worth it. It's like your laugh = this outside force that takes over your entire body. You just can't help yourself. Anyway. I don't know how you got your keys back from me. Maybe they slipped out of my sweaty hands. Even so. You've got one crazy grip for a girl your size.

Man. I really want to bug you. See if you're awake. But you need your rest. It is, indeed, a school night. I don't even know what I'd do. Something to get your laugh going. Maybe I should throw something. If I could just think of something good to say, I'd say it. I wouldn't even be afraid of waking you up. Because:

eyes shut + lying down (doesn't always) = sleeping

~~Your tired but wired friend,~~
~~Hoping for more wrestling in the weeks to come,~~
Good night,
Jake

The next day. Kind of windy, but not enough to complain about.

Back of a Two-Month-Old Bank Receipt on Sean's Desk 7:49 a.m.

Hi. How'd you sleep?

Thought so! Should've opened your eyes. I was awake too.

Not sure. Seeing how long I can keep my mouth shut, I guess.

Don't want to say anything stupid.

I wrote you a letter last night.

No. ~~Maybe.~~ I have to read it over 1st.

Nothing. Shouldn't have told you I wrote it.

■ ■ ■

Margin of Jake's Physics Notes 9:09 a.m.

Stop looking at me like that.

Like what?

Like you want to skewer me + serve me for dinner to your bros.

Well, I do.

Get over it. I apologized. Many times.

You don't get over something like this.

We're best friends.

Were best friends. Now only lab partners. Friends don't do this to each other. Especially guys. We're supposed to be loyal.

We also make mistakes. I was mad. But I wish I hadn't said anything.

Everyone thinks you're so nice and funny. Only reason they don't know the truth is they're not around when you say the things you're really thinking. But I know the real Jacob Jacobsen.

I want the REAL JJ to be someone who KEEPS IN the real stuff. Letting it out = a sign of weakness.

So is doing it in the 1st place.

Then . . . 4 years of friendship down the drain?

Flushed with the explosive shit of a Sumo wrestler who ate Mexican food.

But we live together.

Too bad. I'm done with you.

What about labs?

What about them?

You gonna find a new partner?

No. But I'm not talking to you during experiments. Or any other time.

Fine. Talking + me = trouble, anyway.

No kidding.

■ ■ ■

Dry-Erase Board on Jake's Door 5:15 p.m.

Hey Cocksucker—

Why aren't you talking? Come get pizza. Enough with this silent shit. Your turning into a munk. Its wierding us out.

R + P

Dry-Erase Board on Roger and Paul's Door 5:43 p.m.

It's MONK. As in the bizzaro pianist Hankus played in Jazz last week. And the weird thing about WEIRD is that the E comes before the I. OK, I'll leave you alone.

I vote pepperoni.

White Paper Tablecloth at Pizza π 6:11 p.m.

He hates me. ~~But he was being an ass~~

~~I didn't mean to~~

~~I told him~~

It's too complicated to explain right now.

You sneaky bastards! Just trying to get the "scoop"? So you already know? He told you EVERYTHING?

And you don't think I = most terrible best friend ever?

Didn't he make me sound like the BIGGEST schmuck, though?

True. I guess he's always been kinda cocky.

I know. SO full of shit. Would've done the same thing if given the chance. Probably even worse.

Yeah. As long as it has a hole.

Right. Or Swiss cheese.

So many to choose from!

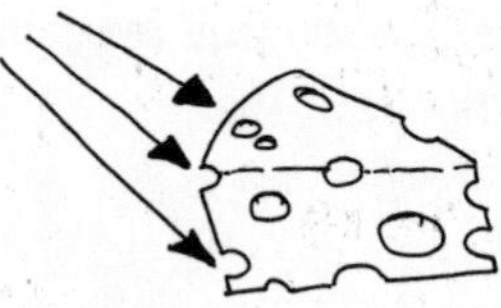

White Paper Tablecloth at Pizza π 6:24 p.m.

It's like . . . Sean told me he doesn't want to talk to me anymore. And I can't blame him—I don't even want to hear my own voice. Might as well just spare EVERYONE.

Writing feels safer somehow. I can catch myself before I say the wrong thing.

White Paper Tablecloth at Pizza π 6:36 p.m.

I know! Did you see her in that short towel? Yeeeikes!

You can tell a girl's REALLY hot when she looks good after she just woke up.

What were they THINKING when they made dorms COED?

Yeah, little did they know they put the biggest PERVS right next to the girls' bathroom!

OK. Across from it too. Can't exclude myself from pervdom.

You actually TALKED to her while she was in her

I can't believe

No, but girls want you to be more subtle.

White Paper Tablecloth at Pizza π 6:50 p.m.

I'd write more, but it's hard to keep up with you guys.

I'm fine just listening.

No. I'm sure.

The more you try and convince me the more I won't want to.

White Paper Tablecloth at Pizza π 7:02 p.m.

You mean pasty-face girl?

Yeah, what's up with her? PJs + robe = p.r.u.d.e.

■ ■ ■

Purple Post-it Slipped Under Door to Jake's Room 11:22 p.m.

Can I come in?

Post-it Slipped Back Under Door to Hallway 11:23 p.m.

I don't know. I'm mopey.

Post-it Slipped Back Under Door to Jake's Room 11:23 p.m.

Maybe I can cheer you up.

Post-it Turned Sideways and Slipped Under Door to Hallway 11:23 p.m.

It's pretty bad.

Post-it Turned Again and Slipped Under Door to Jake's Room 11:24 p.m.

Can I just read the letter? We don't even need to talk about it.

Post-it Flipped Over and Slipped Under Door to Hallway 11:24 p.m.

No.

Upside-Down Post-it Slipped Under Door to Jake's Room 11:24 p.m.

But it's for me.

Upside-Down Post-it Slipped Under Door to Hallway 11:25 p.m.

I know. But I wasn't thinking straight when I wrote it. It was late.

Upside-Down Post-it Slipped Under Door to Jake's Room 11:25 p.m.

You mad at me?

Upside-Down Post-it Turned Slightly and Slipped Under Door to Hallway 11:25 p.m.

No! Not at all.

Upside-Down Post-it Turned a Little More and Slipped Under Door to Jake's Room 11:25 p.m.

Then why won't you talk to me?

Squeezed Along Edges of Upside-Down Post-it Slipped Under Door to Hallway 11:26 p.m.

I'm not talking to ANYONE. Just feel like being alone.

Corner Ripped from Page in Calculus Notebook and Slipped Under Door to Hallway 11:27 p.m.

Why don't you come in. Door's unlocked.

Another Corner Ripped from Page in Calculus Notebook and Slipped Under Door to Hallway 11:28 p.m.

You still there?

Rest of Page Ripped from Calculus Notebook and Waved Back and Forth Under Door to Hallway 11:30 p.m.

HEY!

■ ■ ■

Yellow Legal Paper Folded in Eighths and Stuffed into a Sock in Jake's Dresser 12:12 a.m.

Xandra,

I keep messing up. I thought if you saw me tonight all grumpy, I'd scare you off. But I did that anyway. Without you even seeing me. I should've been more friendly. Sean was right. I'm usually slow with girls. But what're you supposed to do? When you're not sure if a girl likes you that way?

if I...
tell you I like you + you don't like me back →
you won't want to be my friend
if I...
DON'T tell you I like you + you DON'T like me back →
you'll still be my friend
if I...
tell you I like you + you DO like me back →
that's GREAT! but...
I have no way of knowing if that's true + if it's not

I guess there's also this:
I don't tell you I like you + you DO like me back
and the only way to find out is to:
wait until I'm sure + then tell you

Because it's better to have you be my friend than to make things all awkward. But if I really scared you away tonight, then I don't have to think about this anymore anyway.
—Jake

■ ■ ■

Dry-Erase Board on Jake's Door 12:36 a.m.

S—
I left the light on in case you're spinning. But please turn it off when (if?) you come in.
—J

■ ■ ■

Black-and-White-Speckled English Composition Notebook 12:41 a.m.

Miss Me,
I wish I could learn to vanish like you.
—Mr. You

■ ■ ■

Sean's Puke on Carpet Beside His Bed 1:03 a.m.

In the morning. But so dark, it's hard to tell.

Old Calculus Homework Crumpled in a Ball and Thrown at Sean's Head 7:33 a.m.

Gives him paws? Paws!

Old Calculus Homework Crumpled Back in a Ball and Thrown Harder at Jake's Head 7:33 a.m.

Pause.

Old Calculus Homework Crumpled Back in a Ball and Thrown at Sean's Stomach 7:34 a.m.

When did you lose the funny?

Old Calculus Homework Crumpled in a Tighter Ball and Hurled at Jake's Crotch 7:35 a.m.

When did you sleep with Jenni?

Post-it Stuck on Puddle of Puke 7:36 a.m.

When you gonna clean this up?

■ ■ ■

Dry-Erase Board on Jake's Door 12:47 p.m.

DON'T MESS WITH SEQUEL.

WE'VE GOT A PADDLE WITH YOUR NAME ON IT.

—YOUR FRIENDS AT αψ

■ ■ ■

Paul's Upside-Down Calculator 2:08 p.m.

BOBBLESS

Margin of Jake's Jazz Notes 2:09 p.m.

Learn to spell.

Paul's Upside-Down Calculator 2:10 p.m.

BOOBLESS

Roger's Upside-Down Calculator 2:12 p.m.

LOG

LEGS

Jake's Upside-Down Calculator 2:14 p.m.

EGG

BOOBS

Margin of Roger's Jazz Notebook 2:17 p.m.

Got tix for Ψ tomorrow?

No way. You seen the note on my door?

Oh. Forgot. Sucks.

They're calling him "Sequel" now?

b/c he can puke & come back & drink more.

That's all he does these days.

Yup. Scary. What'll you do instead?

Dunno. That's how I ALWAYS spend Friday nights. Need a new plan.

They won't really do anything to you. Right?

What do you think the Ψ is for? They're evil.

Me & Paul will look out for you.

I'm sick of their parties anyway.

I'd hang with you. But already paid for tix. Plus I think Tittiana will be there.

I'll figure something out. Good luck with

Maybe I'll keep Xandra occupied so their room will be empty!

I'm sure you will.

What's that supposed to mean?

I just mean I'm sure you & Xandra will find something to do.

■ ■ ■

Pocket-Size Graph-Paper Notepad with Orange Cover 11:29 p.m.

You're back! Thought I scared you away yesterday.

Only a little. How's the not talking?

easy hard both (circle one)

easy hard both

I feel like I can't respond to people quickly enough. Or whatever I DO write is short + inadequate.

Would it be better for you if I talk to you or write? (circle one)

talk to you or write?

That way we can communicate @ the same pace.

Wait. I've gotta change the music. Been sitting here, tempted to sing along.

You won't even sing?

Don't want any words coming out of my mouth. All I do is mess them up.

I don't know what you mean.

Sorry, I just don't want to get into it. I'm still trying to figure it out. All I know is it feels better to not talk.

What's playing now?

Duke Ellington's Nutcracker Suite. From Jazz class.

I like.

Me too. It's sweet!

Ha ha.

You're humming.

You don't need to say any words to hum.

True. So you like this not-talking thing?

Mostly. Except I hate not being able to say thank you. Like if someone holds the door. Sometimes they don't see my smiling nod. I don't want people to think I'm rude.

Maybe you should carry a sign that says Thank You. You could flash it at people when you need it.

I don't want to draw attention to myself.

Yeah, that could get annoying. So...you gonna show me that letter or what?

What.

Come on...pleeeeeaaase...

Maybe someday. If you stop asking.

All right, all right. Hey, you look sad. What're you thinking?

Stuff.

Like...

Do you ever think ppl are boring?

PPL?

Pee-pul.

Oh...um, I guess. What do you mean?

Like why does fun = getting wasted @ a frat party + random hookups?

What else you looking for?

Dunno. Adventure. Something NEW.

So what're we doing this weekend, then?

Ummm . . . does we = you + me?

Yeah.

Did we have plans?

Now we do. For something new, adventurous.

What's it gonna be?

*That's what I asked *you*. Or can't you think of anything fun enough?*

No, I can.

What is it, then?

Mmmmm . . . a surprise.

Hint?

No way. Just meet me @ the bottom of the south steps @ 9:00 tomorrow night.

It's a date.

Should I bring you flowers?

Only one.

OK. One flour.

■ ■ ■

Black-and-White-Speckled English Composition Notebook 12:53 a.m.

Miss Me,

I wonder sometimes. If you hadn't disappeared in Mom's insides. What you'd look like now. Just like me? All elbows + knees + superstrength glasses? Or would you be the opposite? Since you were a girl and all. Petite + elegant + perfect vision. And how would you handle tough situations? Would you stop talking too? Or would you be a great conversationalist? Totally in control of your emotions. I sometimes think you took all that stuff with you. And that if you were still around, together we'd be able to take on anything. You'd tell me how to deal with chicks + help me with my "emotions." I'd

help you with your math homework + warn you that even dorks like me are selfish bastards when it comes to girls.
—Mr. You

P.S. Don't take this the wrong way. Cause I mean it to be nice. When Professor Swallows gave us this letter writing assignment, I thought it was really dumb. Just a journal in disguise. And we all know, journal = diary and diary = what 12-year-old girls spill their guts in, which = what a lot of the papers in Prof Swallows's class sound like. But you know? It's kinda cool to think about you as a real person, instead of some fetus ghost.

The following evening. With stars and long stringy clouds.

Flour Sprinkled into Xandra's Palm 9:01 p.m.

Pocket-Size Graph-Paper Notepad with Orange Cover 9:03 p.m.

What a gentleman!

*Hey, what's *that* for?*

Duh. What're blindfolds usually for?

But I won't be able to read what you're writing.

It's OK. I don't have anything noteworthy to say.

How will I know where to go?

Hold my hand.

You'll crush the flower!

■ ■ ■

Pocket-Size Graph-Paper Notepad with Orange Cover, Held Up to Train Attendant Window 9:17 p.m.

4 fares please.

Pocket-Size Graph-Paper Notepad with Orange Cover, Tapped Against Train Attendant Window 9:17 p.m.

I can hear.

Ripped Piece of Graph Paper Pushed Under Window 9:19 p.m.

Thanks!

■ ■ ■

Pocket-Size Graph-Paper Notepad with Orange Cover 9:55 p.m.

That elevator felt crazy! Like my stomach wanted to trade places with my brain.

Is it a lot different not being able to see?

*Yeah, everything feels way more intense! And outside I kept worrying that ppl were gonna bang into me or that I'd step in poo. And, um, thanks for making me *stand* on the subway! Jeez.*

I caught you when you tripped.

But still. Not nice.

nice = boring

Anyway, what do you think?

Of what?

Where we are.

Perfect. But too bad we don't have fake IDs.

No, but see? That's the point. Tonight's going to be totally different. We're gonna try out sober fun.

Small Square Napkin with Tippy Top Tap Logo 10:04 p.m.

A Roy Rogers and a Shirley Temple, please. With extra cherries.

Small Square Napkin with Tippy Top Tap Logo Crumpled and Stuffed into Xandra's Purse 10:06 p.m.

See how much nicer ppl are to you when they think you're deaf?

*Or how much *dumber* they think you are! IIII'll beeee riiiiiight baaaack wiiith yooour driiiinks.*

I know! Did you hear that train booth guy screaming @ me?

How could I miss it?

Another Small Square Napkin with Tippy Top Tap Logo 10:10 p.m.

Thanks—and can we have some more napkins when you get a chance?

Jake's Finger in the Condensation on Xandra's Shirley Temple Glass 10:12 p.m. 

Small Square Napkin with Tippy Top Tap Logo 10:12 p.m.

What's it pointing at?

See school?

Where?

Jake's Finger on Window 10:14 p.m. 

Back of Small Square Napkin with Tippy Top Tap Logo 10:15 p.m.

It looks so small next to the lake. Like the waves could swallow it up.

This is the farthest away we could possibly be from campus while still being in the city.

Feels good.

Small Square Napkin with Tippy Top Tap Logo and Roy Rogers Stain 10:19 p.m.

What's so funny? And is laughing against your "rules"?

I guess I'll let myself laugh. There's no chance I could say something stupid just by laughing. But if I tell you what's funny you'll think I'm crazy.

Try me.

Do you ever hear things? Like not the way they're meant to be heard?

How so?

Like the guy behind me just said, "I've got a stake in that company." But I heard it like:

You think that's funny?

Why do you think I'm laughing?

It's not AT me?

Nope.

So do you ever hear things like that?

*I've heard *you* make jokes like that. And Sean. But I've never heard them just out of the blue. Maybe now I'll pay more attention.*

It's the funny.

What is?

That's what me + Sean called it. When we'd hear stuff like that. The funny. Most girls don't get it. Yr the only one I know who does.

*I'm more like a guy-girl anyway. I've never been *girly*.*

That makes it easy to hang out w/ you.

Inside of Unfolded Tippy Top Tap Napkin with Roy Rogers Stain 10:37 p.m.

Hey, what do you think steak man had as a pet when he was 6?

Hamster. But his parents gave it away cause it would poop all over the floor.

Your turn.

Ooh! A game! OK. That lady in the corner w/ the umbrella drink. What was her favorite Christmas present ever?

A pair of denim overalls w/ a rainbow embroidered on the front pouch. After that she only got clothes that she wanted to return.

You're good @ this!

Thanks. I like to play it when I'm waiting for a bus or something. Hmmm...okay. Bald guy on his way to the bathroom. What habit does he wish he could quit?

Counting sheep out loud to fall asleep. It's made his wife sleep in another room for years. But it's the only thing that works.

You're good too!

Fresh Napkin with Tippy Top Tap Logo 10:51 p.m.

Whoa, look @ the clouds!

They're like liquid spider webs.

Man, how do you just come up with stuff like that?

*I don't know. How do *you*?*

I don't.

But you did. W/ the sheep counting.

I wish I could say I made it up. But it's based on ppl I know.

■ ■ ■

Pocket-Size Graph-Paper Notepad with Orange Cover, Leaned Against Wall on Subway 11:56 p.m.

We learned something tonight.

What?

nonalcoholic drinks + the top floor of the tallest building in the city = fun

+ making up stories about ppl

Yes. That too. I didn't know that was fun before.

& I didn't know hearing puns was fun.

Guess we're even.

*Or *odd*.*

Yr gonna out-pun ME soon!

■ ■ ■

Dry-Erase Board on Xandra's Door 12:24 a.m.

It's your turn next weekend.

For...?

Figuring out where we have ODD fun.

Saturday. 3 p.m. Meet @ the big knotty tree.

What's funny?

I always think ppl are saying naughty tree. Like it's always trying to feel ppl up or something.

Okay then. The naughty tree it is. 3:00. Odd outing #2.

See you before then, though. Right? Breakfast?

If yr lucky!

I have a feeling I'm gonna get lucky! Sorry. Didn't mean it like that.

Half-Erased Dry-Erase Board on Xandra's Door 12:30 a.m.

OW! You know what yr asking for, right?

Tell me.

Ever hear of a spin cycle?

Page Ripped from Pocket-Size Graph-Paper Notepad and Placed on Xandra's Pillow 12:49 a.m.

Sleep well.

■ ■ ■

Yellow Legal Paper Folded in Half and Stuffed Under Jake's Mattress 1:08 a.m.

Xandra,

What was that look you were giving me at your door? I couldn't tell if you wanted me to kiss you or not. But when you punched me in the arm, I was pretty sure you didn't want a kiss. You wanted me to turn you upside down, throw you over my shoulder + spin like crazy. Not to mention run down the hall from your room to mine + all the way back. You're just lucky I plopped you down on your bed in the end + not the floor!

But seriously. How are guys supposed to know when a girl wants you to kiss them? It's so HARD (I didn't mean it like that, you perv) because then if you try it + they don't want it, they think you're a creep. And even though I CAN be a creep, I don't want to ever be a creep again.

I wish I had the balls to just ask you if you like me. Or to grab you + kiss you. Or to even give you this letter.

I don't,

Jake

Of course I don't—balls are for something else entirely!

Just as it's starting to drizzle the next day.

Brown Recycled Student Center Napkin 12:24 p.m.

You guys left without me?

We knocked. Paul shouted. You must've been out cold.

Were you shouting "Assface"?

I heard that. In my dream.

Next time try "Jake."

Cake for bfast?

For examination. Roger & Paul say it's menstruation cake.

Sure is what it LOOKS like. Think it's that time of the month for the lunch ladies?

Maybe...if their blood tastes like cherries.

Aww, I can't believe you ATE that!

■ ■ ■

Pocket-Size Graph-Paper Notepad with Orange Cover 2:26 p.m.

You hear what the guy on the radio just said?

Not really. That why yr laughing?

Yeah. The report coming up. It's abt a sports reporter visiting a former Bear in his new home.

*Hmmm...let me guess. A *former* bear. So now he's a...*

Groundhog? Fish? Lion?

...& where'd he move to, anyway? Out of hibernation & into...a townhouse?

Exactly! You totally get it!

This makes you happy?

Yeah. It's another thing me + Sean used to do. Wake up to the radio + laugh @ all the puns we heard in news reports. Lie here in hysterics. Picturing the absurd world we live in.

Will you explain what's going on w/ you & Sean?

I don't know. It's like he used to be brimming w/ the funny. I thought he'd explode from it all. And that I would too. Our heads would pop off . . . + fingers . . . + toes. But he's not into that stuff now. More into making wooden paddles to get himself spanked with + learning secret drinking songs + puking up his lungs.

But what happened btwn you 2? I still don't get it.

Just drifting apart.

There's more to it. I mean, he's ignoring me too. We passed each other @ bfast before you got there. Wouldn't even look @ me. What'd you say to him that night?

What night?

Why being this way? You know what night I mean. Unless you've forgotten whatever it was that made you stop talking?

It was about a girl.

What girl?

Someone he dated.

She go here?

Yeah.

What happened w/ her?

You like asking questions, don't you?

Just wanna understand why yr not friends w/ yr best friend anymore. Seems like a big deal.

I just said something nasty abt Sean's ex.

You apologize?

Yeah. But he'll never forgive me . . . + he shouldn't.

What'd you say?

Just something abt her being a slut.

*That's *all*?*

Basically.

...& that's enuf to kill yr friendship?

The way I said it was BAD.

So...yr afraid you'll say something like that again?

Pretty much.

*Why don't you just not talk to *him* then? Still talk to the rest of us?*

I kinda like being quiet. Not having to gab on the phone/make small talk. Plus, what you DO say (or write) really matters.

Know what you mean. Talking can be scary. And somehow writing feels therapeutic. I feel like our conversations have gotten much more meaningful since you stopped talking. Nice excuse to edit out all the everyday crap. Commenting on the weather/ what you got on this or that test.

It's not annoying? Like yr out to eat w/ a vegan + you can't order what you REALLY want b/c yr sharing?

*No, Jake. What I really want is *you*.*

Ooh-la-la.

Monday morning. Overcast, with a pathetic amount of sun poking through.

Dry-Erase Board on Jake's Door 8:52 a.m.

Where you been all weekend?

You can stay here.

I mean, it'd be OK. We could get along.

Hurry up with your stuff. We're gonna be late.

Then I'll meet you there.

■ ■ ■

Margin of Sean's Physics Notebook 9:23 a.m.

What's up with all the note writing?

I want to remember how to do the lab.

I mean back at the room. On the door.

I told you. I'm not talking.

It's just pretty weird.

You're doing it yourself. Right now.

Because if I spoke I'd get in trouble.

That's what it's about for me. But in a different way.

Jake's Physics Notebook 10:00 a.m.

Constant Acceleration Lab

Materials:

· cart

· ramp

· timer

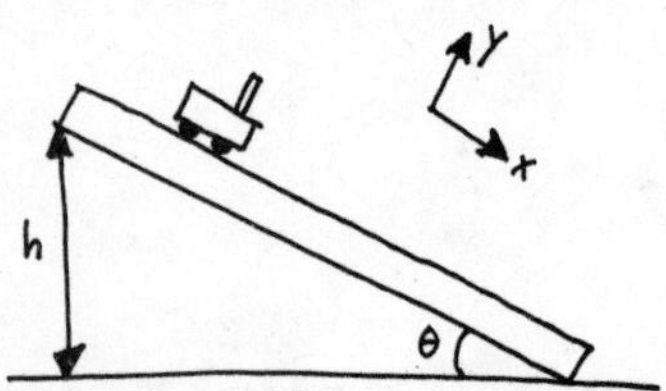

Initial Position x_i (cm)	Final Position x_f (cm)	Time t (sec)	Average Time <t> (sec)	Distance Fallen $x = \| x_f - x_i \|$ (cm)

Margin of Jake's Physics Notebook 10:16 a.m.

What did you get for the 1st one?

Why don't you try it yourself?

We're supposed to be sharing.

You know a lot about that, don't you?

Sean, I'm not apologizing AGAIN. This'll go a lot quicker if we compare results.

I don't trust your results. They'll be tainted.

Fine, then. Give me the freakin cart.

■ ■ ■

Brown Recycled Student Center Napkin 12:22 p.m.

Guy w/ red & white tableclothy shirt, picking out silverware: What's he wish he understood abt his dad?

Why he's made the same turkey sandwich for lunch every single day for the last 20 years.

Brown Recycled Napkin Smeared with French Fry Grease 12:29 p.m.

Speaking of turkey sandwiches, check out the sandwich special today!

Turkey, bacon, lettuce... & tom! Guess it was too much trouble to add "ato."

Kinda nasty, don't you think? Poor guy. Think they chopped him up?

*Hope not. My brother's name is Tom. I like him & everything. But I wouldn't want to eat him on a sandwich. Not w/ turkey *and* bacon. Too much meat! He wouldn't go.*

That's OK. If he's on the sandwich he's in the club.

Whoa! That was totally an accident!

Yr gonna kill me w/ yr puns.

Not KILL you. Maybe make you sick. Of me.

*No, *literally* sick. You'll send me to the hospital. There I'll be, lying in the ICU... & then what'll you do?*

I'll sneak up on you, look you in the eye... + say, "I see you."

Ketchup Squirted on Jake's Glasses 12:40 p.m.

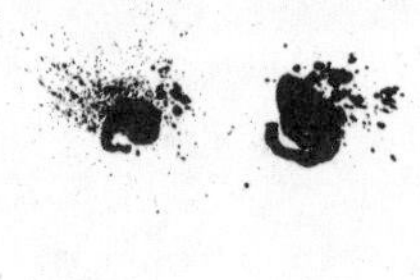

■ ■ ■

Black-and-White-Speckled English Composition Notebook 2:06 p.m.

Hey hey hey... it's freewrite time. I don't know what to say today. There's too much going on to get it all down in a few minutes. And I don't like to leave these things unfinished. Just when I'm about to write something important. And writing the important stuff is risky anyway. Cause what if that guy with the supersmall handwriting that only ants could read looked over my shoulder + saw my secrets? Or what if someone found this notebook? That would NOT be good. Although it seems like my secrets are out anyway. Even with nobody reading what's in this book. But now that I'm keeping my mouth shut, they will only be in here + in my head. Well, I guess I'll just say this: I think Sean has officially lost the funny. And Sean – the funny = grumpy + boring. Those Asswipe Pitchfork boys must've stolen it away. I think he still hears it. He just doesn't want to laugh. Like I'll bet a million $

Sean imagined the mayor sprouting furry cat feet when we heard him say on the radio, "That gives me pause." (PAWS?!) And then this morning we heard a reporter talking about those three armed Palestinian militants. (Watch out! You never know what they might be carrying with that third arm!) Sean glared at me like I was some nutjob when I laughed. But I know—he was thinking the same thing. Because how can you just suddenly stop hearing things that way when you used to hear them every day? So if I = a nutjob, Sean = a nutjob – the uncontrollable laughter. And I'd rather be the full-on nutjob, as long as I get to keep the laughing. Cause what else IS there, right?

Steven Swallows (eew, he does?) is watching the clock. Must be time to stop soon. Looks like superserious cleavage girl is reading today. Hmmm . . . let me guess:

· least amount of time it's taken her to get ready in the morning since she came to City College: 1 hr, 22 mins
· snarfs down spoonfuls of peanut butter when nobody's looking

Margins of Photocopied Student Essay 2:40 p.m.

What did you LIKE about this guy to begin with?

Something less clichéd than "butterflies in stomach"?

What did the rug burn on your back FEEL like?

How do you know his breath smelled like sour milk if you "turned off all your senses"?

I get this "therapist/the rapist" thing. But could be more subtle?

Black-and-White-Speckled English Composition Notebook 2:48 p.m.

The problem with class critiques:

tears + girl reading a personal narrative =
we don't want to hurt her feelings
but . . .
a lot of her writing is sucky + we're supposed
to give an HONEST critique
except . . .
being honest = hurting her feelings
so . . .
people are talking, but what they're saying = 0
I tried to be honest in my comments,
but I held back that I thought this paper = crap
I hope what I wrote ≠ more tears later

■ ■ ■

From: jbloomer@citycollege.edu
To: jjacobsen@citycollege.edu
Sent: Today 5:01 p.m.
Subject: u 'n' me

j-dawg,

hey, whuzup? i just ran into sean and he said u weren't talking. he's pissed at u and if i want to know more maybe u and i should get together. little does he know! l.o.l.

re: not talking. really? like as in not saying anything? that's totally amazing. i mean that must take so much discipline. r u learning sign language or what? anywho, i'd love 4 us 2 get 2gether. maybe u can teach me to sign ;) !!!

call me any time 'o' day or night!

ttyl,
jenni

■ ■ ■

Dry-Erase Board on Jake's Door 6:33 p.m.

Stop by when your back. Rogers got a new sign!

■ ■ ■

Post-it Stuck on "Speed Hump (15 mph)" Sign on Roger's Wall 7:19 p.m.

That IS fast! I don't think I can go faster than 5 mph.

Pocket-Size Graph-Paper Notepad with Orange Cover 7:21 p.m.

Where'd you take it from?

Aren't there lots of cops driving by there?

Wow, sneaky.

I think this is the best of your collection so far.

Yes. STILL not talking.

Maybe you should try writing notes back to me.

It could help you get chicks.

I'm just saying, girls find it intriguing.

I know because I got an email from Jenni today. Suddenly she's interested in hanging out with me.

I don't know. What if Sean saw us?

You're right. It couldn't be worse than it is now.

Where's he BEEN, anyway?

Who's Pointyhead?

Oh—the guitarist in the Beetches?

No kidding. He'd probably cut his chin off if he went to kiss the top of her hair.

So what? You guys put too much value on BIG boobs. Shape's more important.

■ ■ ■

From: jjacobsen@citycollege.edu
To: jbloomer@citycollege.edu
Sent: Today 8:00 p.m.
Subject: RE: u 'n' me

Hey Jenni,

It's true. I'm not talking. As in not saying anything.

> r u learning sign language or what?
No, just writing notes to people.

> i'd love 4 us 2 get 2gether.
Sure, it'd be fun to hang out. Let's meet off-campus though, because…

> little does he know! l.o.l.
I wouldn't l.o.l. too much. He knows a whole lot more than you think.

And…

> call me any time 'o' day or night!
I'd do this for sure. Right now, even. Except remember? I'm not talking. Anyway. It's good to hear from you. What days are good for lunch?

Jake

From: jbloomer@citycollege.edu
To: jjacobsen@citycollege.edu
Sent: Today 8:05 p.m.
Subject: RE: u 'n' me

> What days are good for lunch?
i was thinking more like dinner.

■ ■ ■

Black-and-White-Speckled English Composition Notebook 12:31 a.m.

Miss Me,
Mom's been calling. Left a couple messages over the weekend. She's worried cause I haven't called back. But. How do I tell her I'm not talking? She'll never get it. Talking = food to her. She couldn't live without it. Maybe if you were around you'd be able to call Mom for me. You'd be my interpreter. Like for deaf people. Except you wouldn't need me to sign. Or write notes even. Because. You'd know. Exactly. What. I. Was. Thinking.
—Mr. You

Three days later. Not as nice as they said on the weather report.

Pocket-Size Graph-Paper Notepad with Orange Cover 1:44 p.m.

Cat, I know it's you.

Duh . . . freezing cold hands.

Fine, everyone's hands = cold in the winter. But who else plays "guess who"?

Not talking.

Over a week.

Don't have any plans to start soon.

Try all you want. I'm tough.

Tickling will only make me laugh. Not talk.

Hmmm . . . that might make me let out other noises. But I think I could still control the talking.

Why? Did you have something in mind?

I don't know. You turned me down last time I tried.

Back Cover of Paul's Jazz Notebook 1:57 p.m.

Write somthing to me—quick!

Something has an E.

Something else!

Why are you suddenly writing notes?

You've got Cat after you too! She was pawing all over you. Saying how "admerable" you are. And who knows what else. Your ears are red.

I told you. The girls like it.

Seen Jenni yet?

Tonight.

Man, we've got to try this in front of Tittiana.

Come on, let's go in. Can't be late for Hankus.

Margin of Paul's Jazz Notes 2:02 p.m.

Jakes right about chicks digging the notes thing. I saw it work.

Margin of Paul's Jazz Notes 2:03 p.m.

Try it on Tittiana?

Margin of Paul's Jazz Notes 2:03 p.m.

My thoughts exactly.

Roger's Upside-Down Calculator 2:15 p.m.

I

SEE

BELLIES

Paul's Upside-Down Calculator 2:19 p.m.

hIGh

hEELS

Jake's Upside-Down Calculator 2:24 p.m.

IS

ShE

ELIGIBLE

Roger's Upside-Down Calculator 2:30 p.m.

ShE

IS

LOOSE

Margin of Roger's Jazz Notes 2:33 p.m.

Eligible—good one!

Margin of Paul's Jazz Notes 2:35 p.m.

Jakes are always the best.

Margin of Jake's Jazz Notes 2:36 p.m.

You heard of the apostrophe?

Margin of Paul's Jazz Notes 2:38 p.m.

I know I cant spell. You dont always have to correct me, Professor Jacobsen.

Margin of Jake's Jazz Notes 2:39 p.m.

You just left those out to piss me off, didn't you?

Margin of Paul's Jazz Notes 2:39 p.m.

I couldve. Couldnt I?

■ ■ ■

Dry-Erase Board on Jake's Door 6:01 p.m.

Dinner?

■ ■ ■

White Paper Tablecloth at Pizza π 6:10 p.m.

Hi. You look great! I like the braids.

Oh. I was just drawing a window I saw on the way over. I wanted to remember it. Funny, right?

What don't you get?

No, see? They don't mean THAT plant. They mean the DRY CLEANING plant. Yeah. That's why it's funny.

What toppings do you like?

You can write notes back to me. That makes it less awkward.

This is going 2 be fun! What do U want 2 write about?

Think of it just like talking. Whatever comes to mind.

U start.

What've you been up to?

Oh lots of things. Homework/partying. Super busy w/ sorority.

What were you doing right before you came here?

Balancing my checkbook.

On what? Your head?

On my desk.

Right. ~~But I mean~~ It was a joke.

Oh now I see. Sorry I'm so slow.

Don't worry. I make dumb jokes.

I'll get the pizza.

No, I'll pay.

Want a drink?

Pocket-Size Graph-Paper Notepad with Orange Cover 6:28 p.m.

Also a Mr. Pibb and a water, please.

Thanks!

No, nothing happened. I'm just doing this experiment.

A little over a week now.

White Paper Tablecloth at Pizza π 6:33 p.m.

Keeping busy?

I've got stuff like this all over my notes. All over whatever paper's nearby when I'm on the phone. It's like I've always got 2 keep my hands busy.

I remember that about you.

You thought I was pretty good with my hands.

Um . . . yeah. But I meant how you were always fidgeting with something.

So R U gonna spill the beans about what Sean knows?

I told him what happened. Blurted it out. I shouldn't have.

What did U tell him?

Everything. He knows about that night + the next morning + how you said I was better than him at you know what. I'm sorry. I wish I'd kept that in.

It's fine with me if he knows. That shithead cheated on me I don't even know how many times. Once right in front of my face.

I know. But now that I told him, he hates me.

U don't need him.

The room's so empty without him.

White Paper Tablecloth at Pizza π 6:56 p.m.

What R U doing after this?

Got plans with a friend.

2 bad.

Why?

I was gonna invite U 2 see my room. I moved the bed. It looks better.

Sorry. I would. But I made these plans a long time ago. Maybe another time. I'll walk you home though.

■ ■ ■

Dry-Erase Board on Xandra's Door 7:25 p.m.

Hi. I'm back.

Where been?

Library.

You *never* go to the library. What's so important?

Nothing really. That's why I came back.

You see my note?

Yeah. Wish I coulda gone w/ you. Just grabbed something quick to eat. Find anyone to sit with?

Paulger.

Ha! They ARE such a unit!

*They're both *so* into this note writing thing now. Pretty funny.*

They do it in front of Tatiana?

Yeah. She was w/ us. Thinks the whole thing is totally weird.

Not the effect they were going for.

Not at all. When she left they asked me if I've seen her boobs.

Have you?

Of course. We live together.

Lucky!

Freshly Erased Dry-Erase Board on Xandra's Door 7:34 p.m.

They wanted to know if her boobs are real. I told them they feel like it.

You've FELT them?

No. But I knew it'd get them going.

I have to admit. It's kinda getting ME "going" too. She's BOOBILICIOUS! Though I tend to like em a little smaller than hers.

Thanks for informing me.

No problem. You busy now?

Kinda. But could use a break.

Come over, then.

Scotch Tape over Xandra's Lips 7:39 p.m.

Pocket-Size Graph-Paper Notepad with Orange Cover 7:41 p.m.

OK. So I wasn't @ library.

No. More. Questions.

Scotch Tape from Jake's Lower Lip to Chin 7:43 p.m.

Scotch Tape from Xandra's Nose to Right Cheek 7:44 p.m.

Scotch Tape from Jake's Left Cheek to Brow 7:44 p.m.

Scotch Tape from the Corners of Xandra's Mouth to Ears 7:45 p.m.

Pocket-Size Graph-Paper Notepad with Orange Cover 7:46 p.m.

You sure can look ugly!

Thanks. You too.

Meant that in the best way possible.

■ ■ ■

Yellow Legal Paper Folded in Eighths and Placed in the Bottom Drawer of Jake's Desk, Under Box of File Folders 11:33 p.m.

Xandra,

I knew Scotch tape was good for a lot of things. Wrapping presents. Removing ticks from your skin. But I didn't know it could turn a

cute girl into Plastic Man. Or. Make me want to stick myself to a friend. So she would never go away.
—Jake

P.S. I'm not sure why I lied to you about where I went. I mean, it's not like you're my girlfriend. But. I guess I don't want you to know I was ever attracted to a prissy girl like Jenni. I used to think that hot = dating material . . . + that was all you needed. But tonight I realized that hot – the funny = b.o.r.i.n.g. Plus, you need to have what people annoyingly refer to as "chemistry." Please don't hold it against me. That I just figured this out.

■ ■ ■

Black-and-White-Speckled English Composition Notebook 12:27 a.m.

Miss Me,
Do you think it's weird that last night I had a conversation with Dad where he was responding to beeps as if we were actually conversing? Well. If you'd grown up with me, you wouldn't think that was strange at all. Cause you'd know. Dad's a robot.

The night BEFORE that Mom called again. I had Xandra pick up because I thought it might be Mom. And I don't want her worrying TOO much. Xandra explained the situation. How it's not that I'm ignoring her. I'm just taking time out from talking. And of course Mom freaked. Demanding answers. Xandra said maybe I could send her an email. Then Xandra got a taste of Mom's technophobia. How she can't deal with "buttons + beeps."

Anyway, Xandra was great. She stayed totally calm + was Mrs. Jacobsening Mom all over the place. Then Mom wanted me on the

phone. So I got on. And just sat there. Listening. To her telling me how she just wants to know that I'm OK. But she was going on + on + on. Not giving me a chance to say a word, even if I WAS talking. Before we hung up she said she'd have Dad call me. I didn't even know they were in touch. But whatever. He did call. Like I told you. Last night. And he did this thing where he'd ask a question + say, "Press 1 for yes + 2 for no." And we went through a list of questions. Most of which had to do with am I OK? Things like: Are you eating enough? Sleeping enough? Are there any abnormal lumps on your body? He read them all. Totally straight. I could even hear the pencil jotting down my responses. I bet they were 1's and 2's. Instead of yes's and no's.
—Mr. You

That Saturday. Unseasonably warm, with floppy yellow leaves falling from branches.

Pocket-Size Graph-Paper Notepad with Orange Cover 3:03 p.m.

Tie this around yr face & take off yr shoes.

...& socks.

But it's cold!

Wuss.

What if I step on glass or something?

I'll look out for you. Unless you don't trust me...& then you can just wear yr stupid shoes, I guess.

Fine.

Blindfold stays on till you figure out where we are.

OK. Then spin me around a few times when I get it on.

*When you *get it on*? W/ the blindfold?! Maybe I should leave you alone for a while.*

Aack! I've turned you into a monster!

Jake's Big Toe in Wet Sand 3:27 p.m.

I KNOW WHERE I AM

Pocket-Size Graph-Paper Notepad with Orange Cover 3:29 p.m.

Ow! Your nails! Didn't have to rip that off my face so fast!

Sorry...was trying to be dramatic.

I was right—re: where I am.

But you don't know what yr gonna do.

Lemme guess: throw you in the water?

No.

What, then?

Lie down & close yr eyes.

Handfuls of Sand on Jake's Legs 3:31 p.m.

Handfuls of Sand on Jake's Feet 3:32 p.m.

Mounds of Sand Pushed over Jake's Chest, Pelvis, and Arms 3:34 p.m.

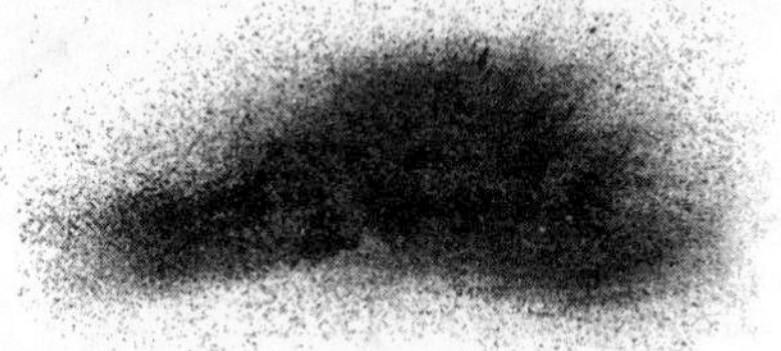

Water Bottle Squirted on Jake's Face 3:37 p.m.

Torn, Soggy Piece of Graph Paper on Jake's Windowsill 4:44 p.m.

Should I bring you flowers?

Only one.

OK. One flour.

New Pocket-Size Graph-Paper Notepad with Orange Cover 4:45 p.m.

I had to save at least ONE page. The rest are all sticking together.

So sad. But it's all your fault, you know.

Oh. OK, Ms. Water Squirter.

That's right, Mr. Running into the Lake in His Clothes.

What. Would you have preferred me to be Mr. Strip Naked + Run into the Lake?

Well, considering that you were carrying me... I guess not.

Shit. I have to dry out all my money!

I never took you for a money launderer.

Ha ha. Seriously. Everything in here is SOAKED!

Ripped Corner of Magazine on Jake's Windowsill 4:58 p.m.

. . . And Pink Post-it Shaped Like Puckered Lips 4:59 p.m.

. . . And Cardboard Ripped from a Six-Pack of Beer 4:59 p.m.

. . . And Back of Bubblegum Wrapper 5:00 p.m.

Pocket-Size Graph-Paper Notepad with Orange Cover 5:01 p.m.

You been paying for things w/ girls' phone #s?

I don't know why I'm keeping those. I never call any of them.

You've got more phone #s than dollar bills.

Not true.

Almost as many.

And hey, aren't Jenni & Cat names of Sean's exes?

Yeah.

You scamming on them, or what?

I actually met them 1st.

Why, the #s bothering you?

*Not *bothering* me. Just observing.*

Didn't get any of them recently.

I told you.

& it's none of my biz anyway.

Why don't you lay the things from yr wallet out here too?

It's nice + sunny.

Mine's not wet. Didn't bring it.

Do you usually go out w/o it?

No. I had a feeling we might wind up getting wet.

Ooh, yr making me tempted to give you a mega noogie.

Oh please. You loved it.

Almost as much as I love giving you noogies.

No. You liked going in the water more.

Fine, yr right. We'll have to do it again sometime. When it's warmer.

In the summer. Maybe wear actual bathing suits.

Summer's too far away.

I know.

■ ■ ■

Brown Recycled Student Center Napkin 6:34 p.m.

There's Sean.

Where?

Little table in corner—don't look yet!

Okay—now.

Still w/ Pointyhead.

Pointyhead?

That grl he's dating. Haircut's all pointy on top. Paulger's calling her Pointyhead.

*Sean's got a new grlfriend *already*?*

He's a smooth operator. Always has SOMEone.

*What's going on w/ him? Does he *ever* come home?*

If so, I never see.

I don't get it.

Brown Recycled Napkin with Spaghetti Sauce Stains Tapped on Cat's Elbow 6:56 p.m.

Hi!

You know Xandra?

Brown Recycled Napkin with Spaghetti Sauce Stains Held in Air 6:57 p.m.

Xandra, meet Cat.

Cat, meet Xandra.

Other Side of Spaghetti Sauce-Stained Napkin Held in Air Behind Jake's Head 6:59 p.m.

Mmmmm . . . you can keep doing that . . . but it's not gonna make words come outa my mouth.

Spaghetti Sauce-Stained Napkin Handed to Cat 7:03 p.m.

See ya!

Brown Recycled Napkin with Lip-Gloss Marks 7:04 p.m.

*What was up w/ *that*?*

What?

Ohhh, Jake, you must be so tense...you troubled boy...lemme rub it all out of you...

Cat likes to give backrubs. Says it's a stress reliever.

*What. Ever. She *totally* wants you.*

Wants to be able to say she got me talking.

Same thing.

■ ■ ■

From: jjacobsen@citycollege.edu
To: aflash@citycollege.edu
Sent: Today 12:42 a.m.
Subject: i'm a big fat liar.

X,

I've been thinking. After flipping through the sad remains of my soaked notebook, I realize I haven't been straightforward with you. So I'm gonna come clean about why me and Sean are fighting. Because I think you might be onto me. And I don't want you to go nosing around and hear the truth from someone else.

Warning: you might not want to be friends anymore after reading this. (That's why I'm telling you in email rather than in person.) I hate myself every time I think about it.

See, Sean's always been better than me with the ladies. Ever since 9th grade, when we started hanging out. But the thing is, he also ALWAYS goes after the girls that I have a crush on. He knows it, too. I've never gotten mad about it. Not to his face, at least. I just figured we had the same taste—but that he always scored because he's much better-looking. I'm like his funny sidekick. I mean, he's funny too. Or used to be. But I have to say, I think he got a lot of his sense of humor from me. The funny. I started it. Yeah, he built on it. But when he used it to charm girls, I heard him saying a lot of jokes I'd made to him. Anyway. I never stopped liking those girls once he started dating them. I tried. Told myself they were out of my league. But I only wound up liking them more. And Sean's . . . well, he's not the most faithful guy. And so there were a few times when his girlfriends would come and talk to me. For comfort. Because they knew I was the nonthreatening best friend. I think I actually DID help them feel better. But. That's how I wound up sleeping with 3 of Sean's girlfriends.

2 of them since we got here. (Yes, you're right, I was "scamming." And yes, I had dinner with one of them when I went to the "library.")

The thing is, every time I "comforted" one of Sean's girlfriends, I'd wish that the girl would leave Sean for me. But they'd always say they only thought of me as a friend. A couple even went back to Sean after he'd cheated on them. Anyway. Sean never knew about any of this. But the night you saw him storm out, it was because I told him about the 3 girls. In fact, I yelled it at him. He'd been rubbing it in my face how I was still a virgin. Which, duh, I'm not—thanks to Sean and his LOVE of multiple ladies. I know he only got so mean with the teasing cause he was wasted. But I needed a way to get under his skin. And I guess I did. But it was a mistake for me to tell him about his exes. Maybe I would've held back if I hadn't been drinking too.

Well, there you have it. I don't know if it'll make you feel better or worse knowing all of this about me. But I thought you should know.

J

Sunday evening. As the first frost forms on the grass beside paved paths.

Long Sheet of Butcher Paper Beside Stolen Sign Collection on Roger's Wall 9:14 p.m.

We got a whole roll of this for group note sessions.

Why do we need it to be so big? Isn't a pad enough?

So the ladies can see. There's a perfect view from the hall.

Now we just need some ladies to walk by. Go take a shower or somthing.

You have a lady right here.

But your one of us.

She can be our bait! Xandra, you act all interested in what we're writing & the chicks will follow!

*I'll act all interested once you write something *interesting*!*

Guess which one of us has the biggest

Wait wait—we have to cover this up so the ladies can't see our plan.

Back of Butcher Paper Beside Stolen Sign Collection on Roger's Wall 9:29 p.m.

As I was saying. Guess who has the biggest schlong: Me Roger Jake?

Me Roger Jake?

But they're just varying sizes of baby carrots.

You pick the shortest guy?

Height has nothing to do with it.

We need a ruler. Jake? Care to step into the closet 1st?

We talking soft or hard?

Whichevers longest.

You guys think this is what's going to get the ladies in here?

Once they see how gigantic I am.

*Not all girls like em *gigantic*.*

My kind of girls do.

Back already? Whats the verdict?

I'm not telling until you guys measure.

I'll go.

Hurry up! The ladies keep walking by! We need Xandra to get excited quick!

I don't think this is gonna work.

You don't need it to work. The ladies already love you.

Mmmm, like Caaaat...

You've seen it too?

Yeah...Jakey-poo got a nice little backrub last night at dinner.

Damn! See?

Fine, so some girls think it's interesting that I'm not talking.

But it's all so phony. They weren't interested before.

I'd take phony lovin any day. Hey hey—heres Mr. Bigstuff!

Go Paul. Then we can post results.

This is a stupid idea. It's not something we should know. You guys just compete against each other.

Then we'll have to assume you're the smallest.

Fine with me.

Oh man, they're at it again next door! Mike's roommate's been away this weekend. I don't think Mike & his girlfriend have left the room once. For food or anything. Plus, she's a screamer!

I prefer moaners.

I like whatever I can hear.

What's taking Paul so long?

Maybe he can't get it back down.

I can't believe I'm standing here while you guys do this.

Come on. At least we're going in the closet!

*Still. Weird. I don't even *care* who's biggest.*

Yeah. This whole thing was about making Xandra (THE GIRL) excited about what you're writing on here.

Finally! Jeez, did you have to finish yourself off, or what?

The ruler wouldnt reach the whole way. I had to do some creative measuring.

Yeah, right. You post first, Jake.

I told you. I'm not doing it.

Paul?

Fine. I'll go. 6⅞".

Beat you. 7¼".

No way. You're both lying.

Hey they're at it again!

We know. We've been listening the whole time you were in the closet.

Paul! I never knew you were in the closet!

Lets get one thing straight: I've <u>never</u> been in the closet.

You're right. That's one STRAIGHT statement.

You two are perfect for each other. With you're puns. Its like Seans still around.

Ooh baby! Here she goes. With the final scream.

Not as good as last night. She must be tired out. Jealous, Jake? Wish you lived in our room?

Moaners are way sexier.

Xandra, are you a moaner or a screamer?

I never paid attention. Probably a moaner. Maybe sometimes a screamer. What about you?

Moaner all the way.

It's not cool for guys to make too much noise.

You guys are so full of shit. How would you even know?

I know what I'd be like.

Are you a virgin, Paul?

So? Roger is too!

Thanks for outing me.

You don't have to get all defensive.

Why? Are you also?

No. Though I've only slept with one guy. My boyfriend in high school. But I was thinking. All this time you've been trying to get girls in here with your penis sizes. When really they'd be more intrigued by the fact that you're virgins.

No way.

Way.

New Sheet of Butcher Paper Beside Stolen Sign Collection on Roger's Wall 10:10 p.m.

HEY LADIES! COME AND MEET SOME HORNY VIRGINS!

I'm not sure that's exactly the way to do it either...

■ ■ ■

Pocket-Size Graph-Paper Notepad with Orange Cover 10:57 p.m.

Got my email?

Yeah. Sorry haven't responded. Wasn't sure what to think.

What abt now?

Makes sense why you did it.

So why not know what to think?

b/c not sure why you told me.

To answer yr questions.

Nothing else?

~~Nope.~~

OK—maybe so you'd feel a little sorry for me.

I actually did. I mean, I could identify w/ you.

How?

Guys usually think of me as "just a friend."

Don't believe you.

They do. Even after making out.

Naw, must be TONS of guys wanting you.

**Wrong*. You see how Paulger treat me. Like one of the guys.*

Sean wanted you.

Really?

Why think he was always getting you to tuck him in @ night?

He was drunk. I was around.

+ he wanted you to take care of him + see him as helpless → so he could pounce.

*I guess it was kinda working. I mean, he *is* really cute...& it's strangely charming how he'd call down the hall for me...& how he'd rub my hand when he got the spins. Ran his fingers thru my hair.*

Thought so!

What?

You liked him back!

Nah.

Admit it. You did.

*Fine. But not in a *huge* way.*

See?

You look disappointed in me.

Just don't get why his act always works.

He makes you feel needed. It's flattering.

Sickening is more like it.

Well, yeah...once he asks you to fetch the puke bucket...

Pocket-Size Graph-Paper Notepad with Orange Cover 11:26 p.m.

There's one more thing I haven't told you. Re: what set Sean off that night.

& it is...?

All started b/c of you.

Yr kidding, right?

No. So I told you he was crushing on you. And when he really likes a girl, he gets possessive. He didn't like that we were hanging out a lot.

But I was hanging out w/ all of you equally. Maybe w/ you 2 more than Paulger. But still.

I know. But he was ready to make a move. I think the only reason he hadn't yet is cause each time he wanted to, he was about to yack.

Could've been disastrous.

Unless yr into barfy kisses! Anyway. That day I was stealing yr keys. Remember?

Like I could forget? Still have scrapes on my hands.

Yeah . . . sorry. Well, when we were in the leaves wrestling, Sean walked by. ~~And he swears I was~~ It's too stupid.

Come on! What?

No.

*You *have* to!*

He swears I was touching yr butt. Which is ridiculous . . . b/c for one thing, I wasn't. For another, I wouldn't dare. Aside from the fact that he was only @ the scamming stage w/ you. So even if I WAS interested, you were still fair game. I didn't touch it. Did I?

Hate to break it to you.

NO!

Umm...yes.

I'm an idiot. I REALLY didn't mean to.

I didn't think much of it. We were wrestling. In fact, I wouldn't have even remembered if you hadn't brought it up right now.

Still. I can't believe I did. After all that.

■ ■ ■

Black-and-White-Speckled English Composition Notebook 12:43 a.m.

Miss Me,

If you were around, there's something very middle-schooly that I'd like you to do for me. Find out if Xandra Flash likes me. If there was a part of her that kinda liked that I touched her butt. Cause the thing is. Even though it was an accident. I'd like to touch it again. But longer this time. See, there are boobs men + there are butt men. Roger and Paul are boobs men. But me? Sure, boobs are nice. I mean, they're great. It's just. I don't care how big they are. Smaller is fine. Not much more than a handful is perfect. I'm more of a butt man. And again. I'm not talking big. Just shapely. Curvy enough to grab on to. None of those superskinny nonexistent ass girls for me. And Xandra's butt? It may be small. But the shape. Is. Just. Right. Sorry if all this guy talk is making you feel weird. But I like to think that you'd be the kind of girl who could handle it.

Anyway.

Would you do that for me? Figure out, with your wily womanly ways, if Xandra wants me to be more than a friend? Cause things are just going so well. And I don't want to fuck them up.

—Mr. You

In the morning, with a snizzling of snow. But nothing that sticks.

Margin of Jake's Physics Notebook 9:14 a.m.

Nice haircut.

Penny did it.

Your new girlfriend?

What's it to you?

Just wondering. You're never around. I don't know anything about you anymore.

I'm living with Penny. Probably the rest of the semester. Then maybe move into Alpha Psi.

She gave you a good haircut.

Just a trim. Past my shoulders was too hippie.

Jake's Physics Notebook 10:11 a.m.

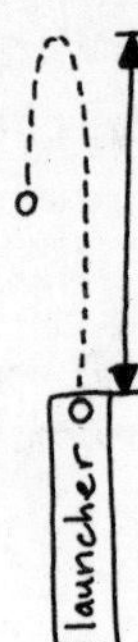

Conservation of Energy Lab

Materials:

· launcher

· clamp

· projectile

· timer

mechanical energy = potential energy (PE) + kinetic energy (KE)

on launch: PE = 0

KE = $\frac{1}{2} mv_0^2$

at peak: PE = mgh

KE = 0

Margin of Jake's Physics Notebook 10:20 a.m.

I don't get this whole potential energy thing. Either an object has energy or it doesn't. Saying it has POTENTIAL to be energetic is just a scientific excuse to make the math work out.

I thought you loved math.

The equations are cool. It's these abstract concepts that get me.

■ ■ ■

Pocket-Size Graph-Paper Notepad with Orange Cover 12:23 p.m.

Ms. Flash, you've been caught. I'm afraid you'll have to follow me to the loony bin. Laughing aloud in front of a newspaper box = crazy.

But, sir. I think you'll understand if you see the headline.

Wow, that's a good one! It's like:

TWO MOTHERS CHARGED OVER
BEER FOR SCHOOL HAZING

I know! That's the 1st way I read it!

Still, I think we'll have to lock you up. Yr disturbing the peace out here. There are students trying to get to class. What if they're late b/c they stopped to stare @ you?

You know I'd never read it that way if it weren't for you.

But look @ how much more yr enjoying the news!

■ ■ ■

Black-and-White-Speckled English Composition Notebook 2:03 p.m.

I'm going to take today's freewrite as an opportunity to discover some new things about my classmates.

Parents met as a nun + a priest.

Frenched her high school guidance counselor.
Before she graduated.

Has only been in one fist fight. When school bully pushed his books out of his arms in the cafeteria. Then punched the principal in the nose when he tried to intervene.

Oh no, Steven! I'm not ready to stop! I'm on a roll here! And now you're gonna make me listen to hoodie man? Ugh.

Margins of Photocopied Student Essay 2:32 p.m.

Her breasts were REALLY the size of globes? Like a regular globe? Or mini?

How do you know she = hottest woman in the USA?

Don't be so surprised. Some lesbians = hot.

That was FAST! She turned straight just from meeting you?

What were you both doing skinny-dipping in the middle of the woods, anyway?

Black-and-White-Speckled English Composition Notebook 2:50 p.m.

What I should've written to hoodie man:

Hey you.
just because . . .
your fantasies + jerking off = great orgasms
doesn't mean . . .
your fantasies = a true personal narrative, which =
this assignment
I think it all = bullshit

Why doesn't Steven call people on their crap? Or anyone else in here? We sit here talking about it like it's real literature. I can't blame it all on Steven, I guess. It seems like he's trying to prompt us to say something. With provocative questions. Maybe I'd help him out. If I was talking. This class is where it's been most frustrating to not say anything. But really. It's a good thing I'm not. I'd just piss people off. And duh. That's exactly why I'm keeping my trap shut these days.

■ ■ ■

Piano Key Stationery Inside Music Note Envelope in Jake's Mailbox 3:43 p.m.

Dear Jacob,

This silent act makes absolutely no sense to me at all, whatsoever. And it's really not a healthy way to deal with what's going on. If you're angry with me, fine, I understand. But you have to understand that I did what I did because I had to. You've got to stop ignoring me. Please give a call or send a note. Anything to let me know what in the world is going on.

Love,

Mom

■ ■ ■

Piano Key Stationery Inside Self-Stick Security Envelope Dropped in Outgoing Mail Slot in Jake's Dorm 4:57 p.m.

Dear Jacob,

This silent act makes absolutely no sense to me at all, whatsoever. And it's really not a healthy way to deal with what's going on. If you're angry with me, fine, I understand. But you have to understand that I did what I did because I had to. You've got to stop ignoring me. Please give a call or send a note. Anything to let me know what in the world is going on.

Love,

Mom

Mom,

This "silent act" isn't about you. Not everything is.

Don't worry about me. This is just something I have to do.

—Jake

■ ■ ■

Brown Recycled Student Center Napkin 6:32 p.m.

Has anyone ever called you Xandy?

No. Just Alexandra or Xandra. Sometimes my mom calls me Xan.

Can I be the first to call you Xandy?

It sounds a little girly, but for you? Sure.

Know why I like it?

No.

Any guesses?

Tell me already!

b/c x and y are my favorite letters. Variables. x + y = xandy

■ ■ ■

Yellow Legal Paper Folded in Eighths and Slipped Inside a Pair of Boxers in Jake's Dresser 11:50 p.m.

Xandra,
Your knees sure do taste good. That's why you came to tuck me in in your nightgown, right? For me to have easy biting access. Or maybe I'm wrong. Since you socked me in the gut right after. Well, I'm sorry, but after a punch that hard, you deserved to be pinned against the wall and given the noogie of your life.

It's funny. I thought that might've been a good time to kiss you. Because it seemed like you were giving me that look again.

but . . .
Sean stumbling in + digging around for clothes + cursing =
mood ruined

Well, that's OK. It seems like we'll be spending lots of time together. One of these days I'll figure out if you like me or not.

And. Something weird. I kinda hope ~~I can feel~~ that spot where you punched me ~~in the morning.~~ bruises.
—Jake

After a few days. With a sky the same color as the snow on the ground. Except the sky doesn't have yellow patches.

Jake's Upside-Down Calculator 2:13 p.m.

ShE

IS

hI9h

Paul's Upside-Down Calculator 2:16 p.m.

5O

IS

hE

Roger's Upside-Down Calculator 2:21 p.m.

5hE

9OE5

4

hIS

hOLE

Paul's Upside-Down Calculator 2:24 p.m.

hE

5I9h5

Jake's Upside-Down Calculator 2:27 p.m.

5hE

9I99LE5

Roger's Upside-Down Calculator 2:32 p.m.

hIS

E9O

IS

BI9

Paul's Upside-Down Calculator 2:37 p.m.

5hE

hO95

hIS

hOSE

Jake's Upside-Down Calculator 2:42 p.m.

hIS

hOSE

9OES

SLOSh

Margin of Roger's Jazz Notes 2:44 p.m.

Slosh! Bet your hose goes slosh for Xandra.

Margin of Jake's Jazz Notes 2:45 p.m.

Fuck off. I'll go slosh all over you.

Roger's Upside-Down Calculator 2:49 p.m.

ShE

8

hIS

9OO

Paul's Upside-Down Calculator 2:52 p.m.

hE

8OO9IES

Roger's Upside-Down Calculator 2:55 p.m.

ShE

IS

ILL

Jake's Upside-Down Calculator 2:58 p.m.

hE

9OES

2

hELL

■ ■ ■

From: jjacobsen@citycollege.edu
To: slutz@citycollege.edu
Sent: Today 4:40 p.m.
Subject: nuts

Sean,

Any preference on nuts for next week? I'm going to the store tomorrow. Join me?

Jake

P.S. I'm still so jealous of your email address.

■ ■ ■

From: slutz@citycollege.edu
To: jjacobsen@citycollege.edu
Sent: Today 5:56 p.m.
Subject: RE: nuts

I can't believe you're asking me to go shopping with you. As if nothing happened.

I'll bring my own nuts, thanks.

■ ■ ■

Pocket-Size Graph-Paper Notepad with Orange Cover 11:15 p.m.

My dad invented that.

Yeah right. Toothpaste?

THAT toothpaste. Sparkle Stripes. It's sposed to appeal to teenage girls. Think it worked?

*I feel so *used*. I just picked the one that looked best.*

To YOU, you typical teenage girl.

Think I'm so typical?

Average as you get.

$$\frac{\text{Northeastern girls + Southeastern girls + Southwestern girls + Northwestern girls}}{\text{number of girls in the USA}} = \text{Alexandra Flash}$$

all the nerdy boys + geeky boys +
loser boys of the USA < the dorkiness of Jacob Jacobsen

Someone's getting annoyed.

Someone likes annoying me too much.

Someone would like to brush yr teeth.

Someone's not allowed in the girls' bathroom.

Someone's going to follow you in there anyway.

Then someone's going to have to smell my garlic breath.

That's what this sparkly shit is for. You should know that, Ms. Average USA.

Sparkle Stripes Toothpaste on Xandra's Toothbrush 11:24 p.m.

Sparkle Stripes Toothpaste on Xandra's Teeth 11:25 p.m.

Foamy Sparkle Stripes Toothpaste on Xandra's Lips 11:26 p.m.

Foamy Sparkle Stripes Toothpaste on Xandra's Cheeks 11:26 p.m.

Foamy Sparkle Stripes Toothpaste on Xandra's Forehead 11:27 p.m.

Foamy Sparkle Stripes Toothpaste on Xandra's Right Ear 11:27 p.m.

Saliva and Foamy Sparkle Stripes Toothpaste on Jake's Face 11:28 p.m.

Pocket-Size Graph-Paper Notepad with Orange Cover 11:33 p.m.

You didn't need to get nasty!

Yes I did. Toothpaste stings yr skin.

Sorry. Just couldn't resist . . . + you started it anyway.

Huh?

The laughing made me get it on yr lips. It's not easy to brush someone else's teeth. You should try it.

Someday I will.

But not mine.

Sure...not yours.

I don't brush.

Yeah right, Mr. My Dad Invented Toothpaste. What's he do @ the toothpaste company, anyway?

Haven't got a clue. And it's not just toothpaste. It's all sorts of dental products.

*You *must* have a clue.*

All I know is: he's been

Scoot over.

Why?

You can watch while I'm writing. But stop breathing into my ear. Yr nose is whistling.

Here, this better?

Gross! When did you turn into a slobbery, ear-attacking wild boar?

When you said I was leaning too close.

So...you were saying...yr dad...

Right . . . so . . . all I know is: he's been going to his office every weekday since I was born. Since before that even. And each night he's made the same exact turkey sandwich to take with him to work.

Hey, that's where you got that from! In the guessing game...

Yeah. Sorry I didn't just dream it up. Yr more inventive than me. But I've been practicing. In English class. For the next time we go → Tippy Top. Anyway. My dad. He dresses real nice in the morning + comes home @ 5:30. And in the middle he's making BIG DECISIONS abt toothpaste + mouthwash + floss. But I've never had any real concept of what GOES ON @ his work. It all seems so boring + mechanical.

The work world sucks.

But that's what we're here for, right? To prep for the boring-ass wrld of wrk?

We're preparing for work. But we get to choose what we study... & hopefully avoid boringness.

Know what you wanna be?

Not exactly. But I know I like writing... & psychology. Maybe a journalist of some sort?

I have NO IDEA what I wanna be.

What turns you on?

Ooh, baby! You REALLY wanna know?

I mean... ~~what gets you excited~~ what subjects do you like?

Math. But no way in hell I'm gonna be an accountant. Equations = interesting. And I like the logic behind them + how they balance out. But I don't wanna spend my life dealing w/ #s.

You want something more creative?

Dunno abt that either. Abstract concepts don't make sense to me. Like in physics. All this energy garbage.

What don't you get abt it?

I GET it. It just doesn't seem real. That there could be different KINDS of energy. Like if I lift you up & drop you thru the floor, sure . . . you're moving + full of "force." But don't tell me that after you land you've generated all this heat + sound + whatever. That it all = what you had BEFORE I dropped you. Sounds like such a made-up concept.

It's hard to wrap yr head around things you can't see. Or feel in yr hands. I've never been into science either. How bout English? You like that?

Writing's OK. But I never know what to write abt. We're sposed to be doing "personal narratives" now. Everyone's been writing abt all these dramatasmic things in their lives. I don't really have anything like that. Which is scary... b/c I have a paper due in a few weeks + it'll be my turn to read out loud.

Teacher know yr not talking?

No. I never said anything in that class before I stopped.

*Maybe *he'll* read it for you.*

1st I have to think of some ooshy-gooshy thing from my life to write about.

*Maybe you'll *like* expressing yr feelings. Could do you some good.*

What's THAT sposed to mean?

Nothing. Just that you might get something out of it.

■ ■ ■

Black-and-White-Speckled English Composition Notebook 12:39 a.m.

Miss Me,

I have a feeling you'd want to be a musician. And you'd know that's what you've always wanted to be. Not a tacky lounge singer like Mom. I mean Mom = an amazing pianist + singer. But you'd = ((amazing pianist + singer) x 10) – the tacky. You'd perform in real concert halls. With audiences that give standing ovations. And not just because they feel like they have to. They'd actually shout, "Bravo!" Because you would've paid attention during piano lessons with Mom. Unlike me, who just sat there listening to the metronome. I hope you wouldn't be too ashamed at how directionless I am. I just can't find anything that "turns me on."

—Mr. You

The next night. Gusty, with more snow on the way.

Pocket-Size Graph-Paper Notepad with Orange Cover 5:59 p.m.

Where are the nuts?

All kinds.

Not chopped.

Thanks—I must've walked right past them.

■ ■ ■

Dry-Erase Board on Jake's Door 6:28 p.m.

You won't believe what Roger got! When your home, come quick!

■ ■ ■

Pocket-Size Graph-Paper Notepad with Orange Cover 8:06 p.m.

Wanna go w/ me? Don't worry. I won't come. Quick OR slow.
Thanks for the reassurance.

Butcher Paper Beside Stolen Sign Collection on Roger's Wall 8:09 p.m.

That's incredible! Where'd you get it?
Intersection of Long & Wood.
How appropriate.
I never knew traffic lights were so big. They look smaller up on wires.
It's heavy. But Paul helped.
How'd you get it down?
Was already down. From all the wind.

So have you guys stopped talking now too?

Just when the door's open.

Any luck yet?

A little curiosity. But no actual play.

Xandra—whats on your arm? Been in a fight lately?

Hmmm...let's ask Jake. Jake, why do I have all these bruises on my arms?

You saying there aren't enough on yr legs?

No.

I guess yr arms just keep getting in the way of my powerific fists.

More like yr killer elbows & knees get in *my* way.

They ARE pretty big, aren't they. Not to be messed with.

Oh yeah? Watch me!

Then watch yrself get more bruises.

Butcher Paper Beside Stolen Sign Collection on Roger's Wall 8:25 p.m.

You guys need to get a room.

Yeah. I hear their's a real nice one right across the hall. a.k.a. "yr" room!

■ ■ ■

Yellow Legal Paper Folded in Eighths and Shoved into a Pencil Box in the Top Drawer of Jake's Desk 11:18 p.m.

Xandy,

I'll pretend I didn't let you win our wrestling match. Because I'm not proud of why I did.

There was this moment when you pushed me with all your might. Used your entire body. And I don't know. Were you doing it on purpose? Your crotch rubbed up against mine. And what else was gonna happen? I got hard. Maybe you felt it when you finally got me on my back and pinned my wrists to the carpet. You were breathing like you ran the mile for gym class + then . . . I couldn't tell if that gloating smile was because you won, or because you could tell I was aroused.

And I was thinking, "Now, now! Kiss her now!" But I thought maybe it wasn't the best time to kiss you when I had an erection. Cause what if you didn't want to kiss me + then we sat up to talk + I had a woody? But my God. Maybe the awkwardness would be worth it. Just to feel your lips pressed against mine for a second. Not to mention other parts.

Oh, man. Not to be too crude, but . . . I've gotta go.

—Jake

The middle of a bury-you-alive-style blizzard, twenty-four hours later.

Pocket-Size Graph-Paper Notepad with Orange Cover 9:27 p.m.

Tonight we have a new challenge.

What?

How to have fun w/o going out.

Play cards?

Bo-ring.

You *come up w/ an idea then.*

Prank calls?

Never done em.

Me + Sean used to all the time in H.S. Fun fun fun!

But wait. Then **I'd** *have to make them. Unless you feel like talking.*

No. We'll work as a team. I'll write + you say.

Okay. But you have to find me someone reeeeeaaaalllllly good to call.

Deal.

Red Felt-Tip Pen on First Page of Jake's Phone Book 9:35 p.m.

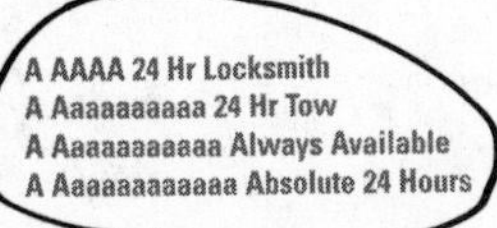

A AAAA 24 Hr Locksmith
A Aaaaaaaaa 24 Hr Tow
A Aaaaaaaaaa Always Available
A Aaaaaaaaaaa Absolute 24 Hours

Red Felt-Tip Pen in Margins of Jake's Phone Book 9:36 p.m.

What kind of service is A Aaaaaaaaaa Always Available? Available for what?

Screaming. (i.e. Aaaaaaaaaaa!)

Red Felt-Tip Pen at Top of Phone Book Page Labeled LOUGHLIN-LOVE 9:41 p.m.

Move arm! Wanna turn page!

Red Felt-Tip Pen at Bottom of Phone Book Page Labeled MALONE-MANASTER 9:44 p.m.

Easy to start w/. Say yr looking for some man asses.

Black Ballpoint Pen in Margins of Same Page 9:46 p.m.

Can't do that. Too little-boyish.

Red Felt-Tip Pen Right Beneath That 9:47 p.m.

That's the whole pt of prank calls!

Black Ballpoint Pen at Top of That Page 9:50 p.m.

I found a better one.

Red Felt-Tip Pen Right Beside That 9:50 p.m.

Can't beat man asses. Unless have baseball bat or something.

Black Ballpoint Pen Under That 9:51 p.m.

Or fist of steel like mine. But really...check it out!

Black Ballpoint Pen in Middle of Page 9:51 p.m.

He's real! MAN Bat

Pocket-Size Graph-Paper Notepad with Orange Cover 9:52 p.m.

Call him.

What do I say?

Whatever you've always wanted to say to Batman.

You call him.

It's tempting to break my silence for a superhero. Tell him how I used to wear Underoos w/ his insignia.

But no. You do it.

Red Felt-Tip Pen on Small White Pad by Jake's Phone 9:56 p.m.

It's busy.

Ooh! Maybe he's online. Making plans to save the city.

Don't you think Bman has a high-speed connection?

Good pt. We'll try him later. Or YOU will at least.

■ ■ ■

Pocket-Size Graph-Paper Notepad with Orange Cover 10:34 p.m.

Try again.

What?

What do you mean, What? Try Batman!

Red Felt-Tip Pen on Small White Pad by Jake's Phone 10:37 p.m.

That was perfect . . . sounding all sincere—"Hi, I'm looking for Batman?"—as if you couldn't just send out the Batsignal if you REALLY wanted to find him.

No name on machine. Hope he still lives there.

Was too good to be true.

Later that night, during a blackout. No heat either.

Pocket-Size Graph-Paper Notepad with Orange Cover Under Flame from Cigarette Lighter 12:34 a.m.

Now what?

Read to me. Bedtime story.

From...?

Dunno. All I have are physics, math, English + jazz textbooks.

I'll get something from my room. Stay here.

Oh. OK. Was thinking of leaving. Going ice fishing or something.

Pocket-Size Graph-Paper Notepad with Orange Cover Under Flashlight and Blankets 12:40 a.m.

It's like we're camping. In a tent. Except in a dorm w/ no heat.

Just as exciting. Pick a story.

Which do YOU like?

They're all good. I have to warn you though. They're pretty abstract. Just pay attention to what he's describing. Imagine the details.

How bout the 1st one?

Blank Space on Last Page of Richard Brautigan's "Revenge of the Lawn" 1:02 a.m.

What think?

You were right. Telling me to just picture it. It's weird. But funny + strangely heartbreaking.

Why heartbreaking?

Cause those poor geese! The grandma thinking they're dead when they're really drunk. Then taking out their feathers! Imagine if YOU woke up from being drunk + someone had taken off all yr clothes.

Depends who it is.

Someone's grandma.

Okay. Bad news.

They could've just woken up w/ feathers + been regular geese w/ a hangover. But noooooo, Grandma took care of that.

I love how Jack sets fire to the pear tree.

Speaking of Jack, don't you think he must work for A Aaaaaaaaaa Always Available?

Definitely. When the bee stings him from his pocket? "##########################!"

This is what talking abt writing should be like. I wish this is how we did it in class.

You mean in bed?

I mean in teresting. In sightful.

■ ■ ■

Xandra's Finger on Jake's Back Through His Shirt 2:01 a.m.

HI

Jake's Bite Marks on the Top of Xandra's Hand 2:01 a.m.

Xandra's Finger on Jake's Back Through His Shirt 2:01 a.m.

OW

Jake's Bite Marks on the Inside of Xandra's Elbow 2:02 a.m.

Xandra's Bite Marks on the Back of Jake's Neck 2:02 a.m.

Jake's Bite Marks on Xandra's Right Side, Just Below Her Rib Cage 2:02 a.m.

Xandra's Slobbery Bite Marks Along Jake's Collarbone 2:03 a.m.

Jake's Tongue on Xandra's Nose 2:03 a.m.

Xandra's Tongue on Jake's Left Eyelid 2:03 a.m.

Jake's Tongue on Xandra's Face 2:04 a.m.

Jake's Finger on Xandra's Arm 2:05 a.m.

TRUCE

Xandra's Finger on Jake's Arm 2:05 a.m.

?

Jake's Finger on Xandra's Arm 2:06 a.m.

T·R·U·C·E

Xandra's Finger on Jake's Arm 2:07 a.m.

N·O
F·A·I·R

Jake's Finger on Xandra's Arm 2:08 a.m.

G·O

T·O

S·L·E·E·P

Xandra's Finger on Jake's Arm 2:08 a.m.

?

Jake's Finger on Xandra's Arm 2:09 a.m.

S·L·E·E·P

N·O·W

Xandra's Finger on Jake's Arm 2:09 a.m.

Y·O·U

1st

Jake's Finger on Xandra's Arm 2:10 a.m.

D·O·N·T

T·R·U·S·T

M·E

?

Xandra's Finger on Jake's Arm 2:11 a.m.

N·O·T

A·T

A·L·L

Jake's Finger on Xandra's Back Under Her Shirt 2:12 a.m.

I·L·L

B·E·A·T
Y·O·U
T·O
S·L·E·E·P

Xandra's Finger on Jake's Back Under His Shirt 2:14 a.m.

T·H·A·T·S
W·H·A·T
S·C·A·R·E·S
M·E

Jake's Finger Low on Xandra's Back Under Her Shirt 2:16 a.m.

N·O...

Jake's Finger Higher on Xandra's Back Under Her Shirt 2:17 a.m.

S·L·E·E·P
C·O·N·T·E·S·T!

Xandra's Finger on Jake's Chest Under His Shirt 2:19 a.m.

O·K...
1·2·3...G·O!

■ ■ ■

Jake's Finger on Xandra's Back Through Her Shirt 3:28 a.m.

XF

+

JJ

=

?

Late the next morning. With snow that reaches first-floor windows.

Pocket-Size Graph-Paper Notepad with Orange Cover 11:53 a.m.

Who won last night?

Definitely you.

How can you be sure?

Snoring.

I don't snore.

Apparently you do.

Well, yr a heavy breather yrself.

How know?

Woke up & couldn't fall back asleep.

We probly traded off. What time awake?

Dunno. Was getting light out.

So you didn't feel anything on yr back early in a.m.?

No. Why? Were you punching me?

No.

Kicking me?

No.

What then?

Nothing. Let's get bfast.

■ ■ ■

Brown Recycled Student Center Napkin 12:20 p.m.

How feel?

Abt what?

You know.

Don't.

Last night.

Dunno. How YOU feel?

*Confused. Was fun. But did it *mean* anything?*

Yes.

What?

I didn't eat enough for dinner . . . + Xandra flesh is tasty!

Ha ha.

What? Why look so serious?

You know what I meant.

What'd you mean?

Is anything different today? Or is that just how we are together?

That's how we are, right?

Right.

So . . .

Just wanted to make sure.

Other Side of Brown Recycled Student Center Napkin 12:46 p.m.

Why? What if things WERE different now?

*What do *you* think?*

I asked 1st.

Not sure it'd be a good idea.

Probly not.

I'd just be afraid of ruining what we have. We're so close... & it's hard to go back to being friends once yr more than that. Wouldn't want to lose you.

Yeah. It'd be really risky.

Maybe someday it'll be different.

Maybe.

Cause if I'm gonna be dating you, I want it to be serious. And I don't know if I'm ready for that.

Yeah. It's like—it'd be nice to have someone to fool around with. But who wants to be tied down?

Would just complicate things.

Sure would.

Small Handful of Snow Down the Back of Jake's Pants 1:56 p.m.

Small Handful of Snow Down the Front of Xandra's Shirt 1:58 p.m.

Large Handful of Snow Down the Front of Jake's Underwear 1:59 p.m.

Back of a Young Republicans Flier Ripped Off Hallway Wall and Slipped Under Jake's Door 2:14 p.m.

Let me in.

Young Republicans Flier Slipped Back Out to Hallway 2:15 p.m.

No.

Young Republicans Flier Slipped Back Under Jake's Door 2:15 p.m.

I was just getting you back.

Young Republicans Flier Slipped Back Out to Hallway 2:16 p.m.

At least you had a bra to protect you.

Young Republicans Flier Slipped Back Under Jake's Door 2:17 p.m.

It was still cold.

Flier for the Beetches Ripped Off Hallway Wall and Shoved Under Jake's Door 2:18 p.m.

How long you gonna lock yrself in there?

The Beetches Flier Shoved Back Out to Hallway 2:18 p.m.

Until my genitals defrost.

■ ■ ■

Yellow Legal Paper Ripped into Shreds and Thrown into Wastebasket 2:42 p.m.

Xandra,

That was pretty BALLSY of you. Sticking your hand down my pants. Though I'm not sure it's actual balls that you felt. More like the tip of my flaccid schlong. And some pubes, I'm sure.

Maybe a few days ago I would've liked for that to happen. Even yesterday.

But things = different now.

I think you were saying today that you like me fine, but good friends + sex = trouble. Which makes sense to me. Because relationships eventually end, right? But good friendships usually last. Except I know for sure that they don't always.

but maybe . . .

me + you = the kind of friends that last forever

and . . .

me + Sean = a different story

because . . .

me + sleeping with 3 of Sean's girlfriends = a deal breaker

But I can't help wondering, if our friendship is THAT strong,

is it possible that . . .

you + me = a RELATIONSHIP that would last forever?

I've heard you're supposed to date lots of people before you figure out who's gonna be your life partner. But what if you meet that person when you're young? Are you supposed to watch them date lots of people and not care? Just wait until you're "ready" for something serious? And when does that happen, anyway? Because don't those oh-so-serious relationships often wind up going to hell? I guess the thing is, I've never seen a truly happy adult couple. But they MUST exist, right? Or what's the point in having a crush this hard on someone? Liking someone so much that you don't care about hottie-hot girls trying to get in your pants? Girls who you used to lust after HARDCORE. Suddenly just not being interested because you think you've found something way better. I mean, I understand what you're saying about how we'd have to be careful if we gave it a shot. But I think we could do it, don't you?

And not that I've had a ton of experience, but dating seems so boring.

dinner + a movie + awkward conversation = y.a.w.n.

Just think. We can make it so that...

you + me = never have to bother with awkward dating again

But if it's not gonna be that way, then you have to keep your hands away from my goods. Because otherwise you = a tease.
—Jake

Yellow Legal Paper Folded in Eighths and Shoved into Jake's Back Pocket 3:05 p.m.

Xandy,
I just wrote you a letter that I really thought I'd give you. But after rereading it, I don't think it'd work the way I want it to.

Instead, let me just tell you this:

Last night when I was lying awake (and yes, you WERE snoring), you rolled over so the back of your shoulder was on top of my face. It was REALLY uncomfortable + kind of hard to breathe. Cause you were covering one of my nostrils. But I didn't budge. Because I've never felt so good in my life. And I thought if I moved, well. We'd never be that close again. Without wrestling. Or biting. Or some kind of fighting.

Plus, your hair smelled really good. Sweet. But not fruity or flowery, like most girl shampoos.

So I understand that it doesn't make sense for us to be a couple or whatever. But the thing is. It's not that simple. I'm not sure WHAT that means. But I thought I should put that out there.
—Jake

P.S. If this note doesn't creep you out, maybe, just MAYBE, I'll show you the one I wrote back on the night you slept in Sean's bed.

■ ■ ■

Back of a Yoga Flier Ripped Off Hallway Wall 8:08 p.m.

Done defrosting?

Dry-Erase Board on Jake's Door 8:08 p.m.

Glad yr here. Have something for you.

Ooh, a present?

In a way.

Give it!

Wait for phone to stop.

I'll get.

Pocket-Size Graph-Paper Notepad with Orange Cover 8:09 p.m.

If Mom—tell: don't worry, I'm fine.

Black Ballpoint Pen on Small White Pad Near Jake's Phone 8:10 p.m.

It's HIM!

Jake's Bite Marks on Xandra's Wrist 8:14 p.m.

Jake's Bite Marks on Xandra's Neck 8:18 p.m.

Dry-Erase Board on Jake's Door, Emphasized with Finger Tapping 8:19 p.m.

Quit it! I'll be off in a minute!

Stay out here.

Pocket-Size Graph-Paper Notepad with Orange Cover 8:36 p.m.

That sure took a long time.

He's a cool guy.

Apparently. But you didn't have to lock me out of my own room.

You didn't have to bite me. Or tickle.

I thought that's just how we are.

Not when I'm on the phone, trying to concentrate.

New rules, huh? What's so important that you can't concentrate over biting?

Duh, it was Batman…

from last night!

Duh, I know. How'd he get my #?

caller ID

Of course . . .

Batman has caller ID.

So do lots of ppl.

What'd he say?

Other than brag abt caller ID?

That nobody's ever called him from that listing.

Course not.

Who'd actually look up Bman in the phone book?

No one, I guess.

But it's pretty funny, why he listed himself that way.

That's not his real name?

No.

How disappointing.

I think it's clever.

What's real name?

Said he'd tell me another time. Wants to draw out the suspense.

Yr gonna talk AGAIN?

Maybe. Gave him my #.

But he told you why he's listed as Man, Bat?

Said he's tired of conventional dating. Meeting girls thru work / the personals / friends. Keeps meeting conventional girls. Thought if a girl actually called Bat Man, it'd be a sign of someone special.

You can't tell what someone's like just b/c they call a "clever" listing.

You thought I was pretty great last night for calling.

I do think yr pretty great. But not just for calling Batman. For all sorts of things.

Okay, well

Well what?

I don't know. You should understand this—it's something new/not boring.

What is?

To make a prank call...and actually find the person's...intriguing.

Talking to strangers = boring to me.

Not sure you've defrosted completely.

I have.

Well, gotta finish some reading for tomorrow.

OK. Bye.

■ ■ ■

Yellow Legal Paper from Jake's Back Pocket, Thrown into Wastebasket 9:35 p.m.

Xandy,

I just wrote you a letter that I really thought I'd give you. But after rereading it, I don't think it'd work the way I want it to.

Instead, let me just tell you this:

Last night when I was lying awake (and yes, you WERE snoring), you rolled over so the back of your shoulder was on top of my face. It was REALLY uncomfortable + kind of hard to breathe. Cause you were covering one of my nostrils. But I didn't budge. Because I've never felt so good in my life. And I thought if I moved, well. We'd never be that close again. Without wrestling. Or biting. Or some kind of fighting.

Plus, your hair smelled really good. Sweet. But not fruity or flowery, like most girl shampoos.

So I understand that it doesn't make sense for us to be a couple or whatever. But the thing is. It's not that simple. I'm not sure WHAT that means. But I thought I should put that out there.

—Jake

P.S. If this note doesn't creep you out, maybe, just MAYBE, I'll show you the one I wrote back on the night you slept in Sean's bed.

New Piece of Yellow Legal Paper Crumpled in a Ball and Slammed into Wastebasket 9:56 p.m.

Xandra,

I was all set to risk everything. Give you that note. And the very 1st letter. And all the others, too. Make a total ass of myself. But now I can't do any of that. Because of one stupid phone call.

Maybe it's good that I didn't give them to you.

cause now at least I know...
you like a masked stranger > you like me
and if...
I'd given you the letters + it didn't go over well + Batman called
+ you were into him → I'd feel pretty shitty

But who knows.

maybe if...
we'd let voice mail pick up + you'd liked the letters →
we'd be naked right now
or at least...
in my bed + your head on my chest + my nose in your hair

and I'd be happy with just that, because the idea of...
touching each other – (fighting or joking) = thrilling
but scary too

It's the scary part that I'm not ready for.
—Jake

P.S. Please pretend you forgot that I said I was going to give you something tonight.

P.P.S. I don't know why I'm even writing this. It's not like I'm going to actually give it to you.

Barely any snow without footprints after only a day.

Printer Paper Folded in Quarters, Taped on Bottom Edge, and Slipped Inside Jake's Physics Notebook 7:54 a.m.

Sean,

On the radio they were just talking about presidential balls. Of course, I was like: Man, I wish MINE were PRESIDENTIAL. Then I thought how we could really use those for our experiment today. They'd for sure hold the most energy. Don't you think? Presidential nuts?

The other thing I was thinking was how I wanted to laugh about it with you. This has been going on way too long. Will you at least TRY being friends?

—Jake

■ ■ ■

Margin of Jake's Physics Notes 9:09 a.m.

Didn't recognize you at first.

Been like this for a week.

Haven't seen you in a week. Penny did it again?

Yup.

You look so preppy.

Clean cut.

That too. It's just shocking. Never known you with short hair.

Margin of Jake's Physics Notes 9:33 a.m.

What kinds of nuts did you bring?

Mine. And you can't touch them.

See? You DO still have the funny.

Just stating the obvious.

Printer Paper Folded in Quarters and Taped on the Bottom Edge Handed to Sean Under Desk 9:37 a.m.

Read Me

Unfolded Printer Paper Handed Back to Jake Under Desk 9:40 a.m.

Sean,

On the radio they were just talking about presidential balls. Of course, I was like: Man, I wish MINE were PRESIDENTIAL. Then I thought how we could really use those for our experiment today. They'd for sure hold the most energy. Don't you think? Presidential nuts?

The other thing I was thinking was how I wanted to laugh about it with you. This has been going on way too long. Will you at least TRY being friends?

—Jake

NO WAY.

Jake's Physics Notebook 10:16 a.m.

Measuring Calories Lab

Materials:

· ring stand

· large metal can (coffee)

· small metal can (soda)

· thermometer
· water
· 1 cork
· 1 needle
· various kinds of nuts

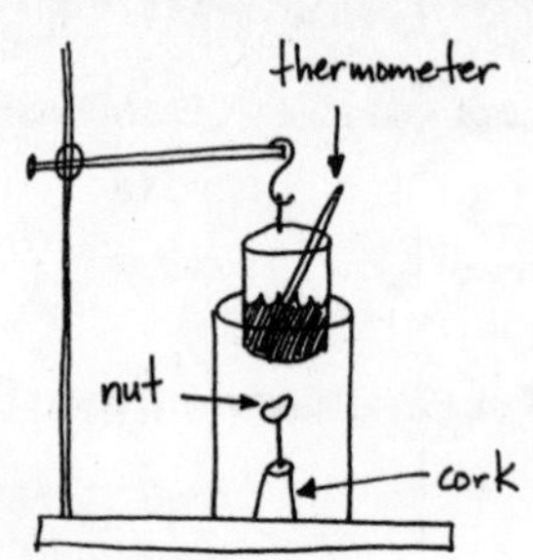

$$\text{nut energy} = \frac{\text{mass of water x change in temp}}{\text{mass of nut x 100}}$$

Type of Nut	Nut Mass (g)	Water Mass (g)	Initial Temp	Final Temp	Change in Temp (°C)	Nut Energy (Cal/g)
Peanuts						
Almonds						
Walnuts						
Pine Nuts						
Jake's Nuts	Yes. Yes he is.					

Margin of Jake's Physics Notes 10:35 a.m.

Why do you have to be like that?

OK. Yes. I know WHY.

But can't you give me another chance?

Cause we got each other so well.

Fine. Then burn the next nut.

■ ■ ■

Singe Marks from Cigarette Lighter on Three-Year-Old Photograph of Jake and Sean 12:23 p.m.

Permanent Marker on Back of Burnt Photograph, Tossed on Sean's Unmade Bed 12:25 p.m.

How much energy WAS there (Cal/g)?

■ ■ ■

Black-and-White-Speckled English Composition Notebook 2:04 p.m.

Today everything = crap. The kind that burns as it drizzles out of your crack.

When I woke up I was looking forward to guessing stuff about more people in here. The girl who everyone thinks is a boy. The guy who dots his periods and i's so hard you can hear it across the room. But now all I wanna do is lie down + stop. Stop thinking. About how me + Sean are REALLY never gonna be friends again. How he still has the funny, but doesn't want to enjoy it with me. Which is probably worse than if he'd lost it entirely. How I haven't eaten since breakfast. Because I spent lunch setting fire to a picture + stomping around my room. How I'm not telling Xandra about it because ~~we're fighting~~ ~~she's being annoying~~ she's all "intrigued" by this Batman character + I hate it + she knows it. And it wouldn't be so bad if she didn't KNOW it. And if it wasn't my own damn fault that she even TALKED to this guy.

The last thing I want to do right now is critique someone's goddamn paper. Maybe I'll just leave my copy blank.

Margins of Photocopied Student Essay 2:47 p.m.

■ ■ ■

Butcher Paper Beside Stolen Sign Collection on Roger's Wall 7:47 p.m.

Seen Sean lately?

At Pitchfork Sat night.

He totally cleaned up.

Looks like Pointyhead's giving him a makeover.

Yeah. Wierd. Its like he's loosing his style.

Losing his style & lots of dinners.

Still?

I think it's just how he lives now. Eat drink puke drink puke...

You guys still lab partners?

Yeah. It's pretty awful. I've been trying to be friendly. But I think I'm done. He makes me feel like such a humungous asshole. Like you could fit a watermelon between my cheeks.

You <u>did</u> sleep with 3 of his girlfriends.

I guess I AM pretty terrible.

Shit, I didn't mean to make you feel bad. Hey—look at him, anyway. You wouldn't want to be his friend. He's a mess.

Exept for his hair.

Thanks, Paul. I'm trying to make him feel better.

You're right. I probably WOULDN'T like hanging out with him much these days. But wish I could make that decision myself. Now I don't even have a choice.

■ ■ ■

Yellow Legal Paper Folded in Eighths and Pushed Inside a Glove Whose Partner Was Lost at the Movies 10:03 p.m.

Xandy,
More than anything. I want to hear you laugh. Right now. You've become my new best friend.

once upon a time . . .
me + sean = lots of laughing
now . . .
me + sean = lots of anger
me + lots of anger = – sean
me – sean = sad
sad + you = laughing again
sad – you = sad^3

—Jake

■ ■ ■

Dry-Erase Board on Xandra's Door 10:45 p.m.

Hi.
I'm on phone.
I'll wait.
Come back in 15?
OK.

■ ■ ■

Dry-Erase Board on Xandra's Door 11:01 p.m.

Off yet?

Just about to hang up.

Stay.

Dry-Erase Board on Xandra's Door 11:06 p.m.

What hiding behind yr back?

■ ■ ■

From: aflash@citycollege.edu
To: jjacobsen@citycollege.edu
Sent: Today 11:52 p.m.
Subject: dangerously close

j

when you aimed the plunger at my face and chased me around the girls' bathroom, i thought, thank god things are finally back to normal.

~x~

From: jjacobsen@citycollege.edu
To: aflash@citycollege.edu
Sent: Today 11:57 p.m.
Subject: RE: dangerously close

> thank god things are finally back to normal.
By normal, do you mean that I mistook your face for a clogged toilet? If so, then you're right.

■ ■ ■

Dry-Erase Board on Jake's Door 12:34 a.m.

I just remembered. You had something for me.

No.

The other night. You said you did.

Dunno what yr talking abt.

Yes you do.

I had something. But dunno what did w/ it.

Well anyway. Glad to see you smiling again. Was afraid yr mouth was frozen too.

It was. But I'm so hot, I'm capable of melting anything.

■ ■ ■

Black-and-White-Speckled English Composition Notebook 12:51 a.m.

Miss Me,

I wish Mom would stop freaking out. This would be a whole lot easier if she'd just give in + use email. There'd be no more frantic voice mail messages asking if I'm sure I'm OK. I could just send a reassuring note through cyberspace. And she'd see. It's the same old me. Maybe I should send another letter via snail mail. Not like I owe her explanations or anything. I never got one from her.

isn't the way it works . . .
communication from one person =
communication from another
but . . .
communication from one person x 0 ≠
communication from another

I wish you were here to help explain this to her. You'd know just the right words to use. To keep her from getting defensive. I sometimes think she wishes you were around too. Especially when I was little. Like how she'd already bought the double stroller before I was born. And kept it anyway. Then the bunk beds. Plus, as I got older she'd say things about how she never knew what I was thinking. That boys keep it all in. Implying, I thought, that girls don't. And that YOU wouldn't. That you would've been an easier child to interpret. Maybe she wishes I'd been the one to disappear without a trace. Which. I have to say. Is so bizarre. Don't you think? That with science as advanced as it is, they couldn't figure out where the hell you went? Not out of Mom, not anywhere inside her. Nothing.

There's no equation for that.

—Mr. You

After a few days of snow melting, freezing, and melting again.

Margins of Jake's Jazz Notes 2:12 p.m.

What were you doing with Xandra last night? Door shut for so long!

Just hanging out.

Come on. No smoochy smooch-smooch?

Some punchy punch-punch.

You guys need to knock that off & admit that what you really want to do is get in the sack.

We don't.

Your RE-DICK-ULOUS.

My RE-DICK-ULOUS what?

You are RE-DICK-ULOUS.

Well, you're RE-COCK-ULOUS.

You're both RE-SCHLONG-ULOUS.

Don't be RE ULOUS.

■ ■ ■

Pocket-Size Graph-Paper Notepad with Orange Cover 8:07 p.m.

Debit.

Thanks.

That's pretty weird.

■ ■ ■

From: jjacobsen@citycollege.edu
To: aflash@citycollege.edu
Sent: Today 10:19 p.m.
Subject: where are you?

I've been looking for you all night! Are you in your room and not answering your door? Are you on the phone again? Blahblahblah-ing?

From: aflash@citycollege.edu
To: jjacobsen@citycollege.edu
Sent: Today 10:35 p.m.
Subject: RE: where are you?

i'm in the library. studying for psych. tatiana's hanging with some guy in our room. they seemed like they wanted privacy. too bad for paulger. anyway, if she's not answering the door, i bet that's *good* news for her.

you still online?

From: jjacobsen@citycollege.edu
To: aflash@citycollege.edu
Sent: Today 10:37 p.m.
Subject: RE: where are you?

> you still online?
Yeah, I'm here. Let's chat.

aflash: why were you looking for me so frantically anyway?

jjacobsen: Wanted to tell you abt this thing that happened. When I went to the supermarket for choc pudding. (Had this major craving.)

aflash: *mmmmm*...have any left?

jjacobsen: Left whats? Hands? Yes, one. And a foot too.

aflash: that was a s t r e t c h.

jjacobsen: How can you tell I'm stretching? You can't even see me.

aflash: you *know* what i mean.

jjacobsen: I know you *are* mean.

aflash: you stealing my method of *emphasizing* words? if so, you are *such* *dead* *meat* when i get back.

jjacobsen: What kind? *salami*? *turkey*? *corned beef*? or my *favorite*...*tom*?

aflash: *uggggh*. just get to the point already—what happened at the store?

jjacobsen: Tooth things:
Oneth: Yr only groaning cause you love it.
Tooth: The store...it was really weird. The cashier lady started talking to me abt how she's a chocolate fiend. Remember...I was buying choc pudding. And she told me her

bfriend doesn't like chocolate. And she just doesn't get how anyone could not like chocolate. That it makes her feel orgasmic. Well, not EXACTLY orgasmic, she said. But the way she feels AFTER sex. And I just stood there as she went on and on.

aflash: did she know you weren't talking?

jjacobsen: Yeah. I had to write her notes abt how I was paying.

aflash: she knew she had a captive audience.

jjacobsen: I guess. But why'd she think I'd care?

aflash: it doesn't matter if you cared. a man who listens is hard to find.

jjacobsen: Well, whatever the reason, she totally WENT OFF on chocolate. And then she launched into this monologue about the store. She told me the strangest pairs kept coming in. And of course, I immediately picture lumpy, misshapen pears.

aflash: but she meant...

jjacobsen: Couples. Strange couples. As in, one likes choc and the other hates it. And they fight over things like ice cream flavors at the register.

aflash: so...her meaning wasn't ap-pear-ent?

jjacobsen: You mean like a mom or a dad?

aflash: ooh, corny! i'm going to hurl all over this keyboard.

jjacobsen: That bytes.

■ ■ ■

Dry-Erase Board on Xandra's Door 12:02 a.m.

Hi. Figured you'd be back by now. Wanna tuck me in?

Read me a story?

Sorry...I'll be off in a min.

Aren't you sick of the phone yet?

I'll come by later...

■ ■ ■

Black-and-White-Speckled English Composition Notebook 12:14 a.m.

Miss Me,

The phone sucks. All it does is eat up people's time. Isn't it better to actually BE with people? Face to face? I think girls like the phone better than guys. But I hope that if you were around, you'd hate it just as much as me. Or at least you wouldn't be gabbing on it all the time. Even if you enjoyed it. You'd use it sparingly.

—Mr. You

■ ■ ■

Dry-Erase Board on Jake's Door 12:58 a.m.

Hey.

Hi.

Was there a reason you wanted to see me?

Just to hang out.

Oh. Well...can't be too long.

Test early in a.m.

Pocket-Size Graph-Paper Notepad with Orange Cover 1:02 a.m.

Yr on the phone a lot these days.

Guess so.

W/ parents?

A little. More w/ that guy.

Which guy?

Prank call guy.

BATMAN?

Yeah...but you know, it's not his real name.

What IS his real name?

Still hasn't said.

Learning more "intriguing" things?

Yeah...I'm...

I'm what?

Going on a date w/ him. Friday.

Why'd that seem like a confession?

It didn't.

Oh. O-KAY.

Don't be an idiot. It wasn't a confession.

It was. You know I'm right.

■ ■ ■

Yellow Legal Paper Ripped to Bits and Buried in Wastebasket Under Other Discarded Papers 1:11 a.m.

Xandra,

I shouldn't be freaking out. Right?

1 date = not a big deal

But shit. I already hate this guy. And I don't even know his name.

—Jake

A frozen Friday night.

Dry-Erase Board on Xandra's Door 9:11 p.m.

You—

Stop by when you get back.

—Me

■ ■ ■

Butcher Paper Beside Stolen Sign Collection on Roger's Wall 9:34 p.m.

This writing notes thing is not getting us any chicks.

Plus Tittiana has a boyfriend.

But I like it when you write with me.

Where's Xandra? Don't you like it better when she's doing the writing?

On a date.

Your lying.

Nope.

With?

Batman.

Really. Who?

For real. It's some guy I dared her to call in the phone book. Listed as Man, Bat.

She's cheating on your ass with Batman?

We're just friends.

Whatever.

I bet you know if she's a moaner or a screamer.

No idea.

But you hope moaner.

Fuck off.

Sorry. Come on. Don't be upset. We're playing. Want to come to $\alpha\psi$?

We'll write notes with you.

Thanks . . . but I'll pass.

We're going beer goggling.

Huh?

My idea. Take off our glasses & drink . . . & be happy with ugly chicks!

Mmmm . . . tempting. But still. I think I'll stay here.

& do what?

Don't know yet. Sit around writing notes + wait for the chicks to flock?

■ ■ ■

Yellow Legal Paper Folded in Eighths and Placed Inside a Self-Stick Security Envelope, Along with Seven Other Pieces of Yellow Legal Paper Folded in Eighths 10:18 p.m.

Xandy,

time – you = s.l.o.w.

—Jake

Front of Self-Stick Security Envelope 11:15 p.m.

X,
In here is something you've been wanting to see.
Plus some extras.
Open + read + please be kind.
—J

■ ■ ■

Dry-Erase Board on Jake's Door 12:42 a.m.

Hey there.

Yr back! I missed you.

What were you doing all this time?

Nothing really.

Sad way to spend Fri night.

Kinda. But got something done I've been meaning to do.

What?

Show you later. Come in.

Pocket-Size Graph-Paper Notepad with Orange Cover 12:51 a.m.

How was yr DATE?

He showed up w/roses!

Sounds CHEESY to me.

Sometimes girls like a little cheese. Makes you feel wanted.

As long as it's not cheddar. You could cut yrself if it's too sharp!

Never really liked cheddar.

How bout gouda? It's so good-a.

Certainly is.

I bet his cheese is the cheddar kind.

I don't know. The roses were nice.

Did you get to ride in the Batmobile?

He's got a Beetle. New one, with the flower still inside... & a GPS system he added.

So he can respond quickly to trouble?

So he can get us to the restaurant w/o looking up directions.

Find out his real name?

Don't want to tell you.

Ooh, now I need to know.

No.

Come on, I NEED to know!

You have to promise to turn off your pun sensors.

I'll try.

Lester.

Bad. But not terrible.

Liddle-Bhutt.

What?

Last name: Liddle-Bhutt.

Parents hyphenated, huh?

Yeah, both took that name when got married. His dad's real progressive.

I guess.

Yeah.

See how mature? Not laughing.

Proud of you.

Small-Tush.

Go ahead. Punch me. I deserve it.

Hey! You said I could.

Didn't say I wouldn't punch you back.

Dry-Erase Board on Jake's Door 1:10 a.m.

Yr going to bed already?

~~It's just, I wanted to~~

Never mind. See you tomorrow.

■ ■ ■

Yellow Legal Paper Folded in Eighths and Shoved into Ripped-Open Self-Stick Security Envelope 1:16 a.m.

Xandy,
I think giving you all of the letters tonight would've seemed desperate. And desperation = no way to get a girl. I really almost did it just before you left my room. But I think I have a BETTER idea now:

we'll go to the Tippy Top Tap + play your guessing game
then . . .
I'll ask about the guy in front of you + you'll have to guess who he has a major crush on
you'll look at me + know exactly what I mean
and . . .
I'll = irresistible

How could you possibly turn down charm like that?
—Jake

Another brisk morning. With icicles that could kill.

Butcher Paper Beside Stolen Sign Collection on Roger's Wall 11:30 a.m.

How was beer goggling?

What's that?

Roger, tell her.

*You guys are *awful*!*

Yes, *completely* awful! But I'm strangely intrigued.

Come over here & write it. And open the door...maybe my fascination will be obvious...and lure some girls in here...

So...you were dancing...

We each found a girl. They seemed pretty into us.

Don't ask me what they looked like. I couldn't see them and I don't even remember after all those beers.

Get any play?

More than I ever dreamed!

Liar. You've dreamed of way more.

True. But more than I've ever gotten in public.

Did you go home with them?

That's the problem. We told them we'd walk them to their dorms. But we both had to pee like motherfuckers & the line was huge.

They were waiting for us on the couch for a while. We finally decided to piss outside even though it was freezing.

By the time we got back in it was too late. One of them was passed out & the other left with another guy.

Damn! So close!

At least we woke up to the screamer.

That again.

What? There's never been another time in my life that I've gotten to hear people doing it live.

Not even your parents?

OK, yes. My parents. But that's nasty.

Me too. Its totally wrong. I used to hear the matress squeeking.

I know. It *is* pretty awful. But see? You've heard ppl doing it before.

I've never heard mine.

Lucky! They must be good at keeping quiet.

So good that they don't do it.

Everyone's parents do.

Not mine.

How do you know?

I just do.

How?

They've slept in separate beds since I was little.

Why?

Something about my dad counting sheep out loud.

Nobody does that.

My dad does.

Still. Your mom must've snuck back in & you just didn't notice. (And hey, don't think I didn't notice that sheep counting thing.)

I'm telling you. I'm sur

Shit! I've gotta go.

What's wrong?

See the lady knocking on my door?

That's what.

■ ■ ■

Dry-Erase Board on Jake's Door 11:56 a.m.

What are you doing here?

Let's go in my room.

Pocket-Size Graph-Paper Notepad with Orange Cover 12:00 p.m.

You drove all the way out here just to check up on me?

I TOLD you. It's not about that. Didn't you get my response to your letter?

How many times do I have to tell you I'm OK?

Yeah, but my friend told you on the phone. And I'm guessing Dad told you.

I just don't FEEL like talking. That's all.

Everything's the same except for that.

Not around. He's been living with his new girlfriend.

I don't really know her.

Yeah, I'm pretty hungry.

There's a place down the street.

Paper Place Mat with Joe's Diner Logo 12:27 p.m.

You've been talking to Dad?

It's going OK?

So maybe my not talking has been good.
It's brought you two together.

I know. I didn't mean together in that way.

How's Curtis?

Coffee from the Bottom of Jake's Mug on White Paper Place Mat with Joe's Diner Logo 12:45 p.m.

Pocket-Size Graph-Paper Notepad with Orange Cover 1:17 p.m.

Thanks for lunch.

Yes. I promise I'll let you know if I need help.

Bye.

■ ■ ■

Pocket-Size Graph-Paper Notepad with Orange Cover 2:36 p.m.

U.g.h.

You didn't know she was coming?

Nope. Surprise!

How'd it go?

OK I guess. As well as it could go. She just doesn't stop talking. She says she came to check up on me. But I think it was really so she could talk talk talk w/o interruption.

About?

The piano tuner. Curtis.

What's the deal w/ him?

She's living w/ him. They're boyfriend + girlfriend.

Didn't know yr parents were divorced.

They're not. Yet. She left a few months ago.

It's nice that she cares enuf to drive out & see what's up w/ you. You can't blame her for all the talking. I mean, it's not like you were gonna contribute much.

She could pause a little. For me to write notes. I just tune her out after a while.

*Not *everyone's* gonna get it, Jake. It *is* unusual.*

She could've at least warned me she was coming to visit.

True. But you have to admit. The sentiment was right.

Sure. She can be so ANNOYING though.

All the talking?

More than that.

She didn't seem so bad to me.

You've never had to live w/ her.

What'd she do?

Stuff.

*Oh yeah. I know what you mean. Stuff is *baaad*.*

Just dumb things.

Like...

Leaving the sprinklers on when it's raining.

A mistake anyone could make.

But she's like that w/ EVERYTHING. Gets her naturally curly hair permed. Puts sugar AND honey in her tea. Totally redundant.

*Tell me more, *Jacob Jacobsen*...*

Yeah, see? I guarantee you that name was NOT my dad's idea. And how bout those animal prints?

*It's true. Her style *could* use some work.*

tiger coat + leopard bag + zebra shoes = fashion faux pas

■ ■ ■

Black-and-White-Speckled English Composition Notebook 12:20 a.m.

Miss Me,

I wish more than ever before that you existed. Nobody nobody nobody will ever get what it's like to deal with Mom like you would. Even my closest friends will never get it. Because how can I TELL them what it's like to come home from school + smell sex in the living room . . . + know it's not from your mom + dad. Which would be bad enough. There's no explaining that. You have to experience it to know what it's like. Which I'm sure you would've. The problem is:

you don't exist + I'm looking for empathy from you
and . . .
seeking empathy from someone who doesn't exist = 0 help

Do you ever miss ME this much? In your prefetal world?
—Mr. You

On Monday. So cold that snot crystallizes in nostrils.

Burnt Photograph Slapped on Top of Jake's Physics Notebook 8:57 a.m.

How much energy WAS there (Cal/g)?

A whole fuckin lot. Then you burned me. And now it's gone.

Margins of Jake's Physics Notebook 8:58 a.m.

Didn't know you ever got that.

When were you in the room?

Margins of Jake's Physics Notebook 9:10 a.m.

~~You got another haire~~

■ ■ ■

Black-and-White-Speckled English Composition Notebook 2:12 p.m.

Hello, freeeeeewrite! Let me begin by saying I think it's entirely possible that Steven Swallows GETS the funny. A college professor. Who would've thought? Even as I'm writing this, I'm having trouble holding in my laughter. I'm not sure everyone noticed. But he knows I did. For sure.

He was going on about some author visiting campus to give a reading. (Yawn.) And he recommends we read part of her book over the next week. And that if she touches us, we should be sure to come early. That's right, boys. Forget what all the ladies say about wanting you to last. This woman wants you to come EARLY. Simply from TOUCHING you. Well. I think Steven realized what it sounded like as he was saying it because he kinda slowed down just before the come early part. Then he nervously glanced around the room. Mostly he got brain-dead stares back. But not from me. He saw me ready to burst. And he just gave a throat-clearing "Well then!" and moved on. I'm shocked. I didn't think grownups heard things that way. Too immature for their ears. I guess I was wrong.

■ ■ ■

Butcher Paper Beside Stolen Sign Collection on Roger's Wall 4:14 p.m.

Sean officially = Pointyhead

What do you mean?

Penny finished the hairstyle. His = hers.

We've totally lost him.

Shit. The door's been closed. No girls are seeing us write!

Not like its been working anyway.

Why are you still writing, then?

Don't know. Maybe cuz you like it. Seems like you could use things that make you happy these days.

■ ■ ■

Dry-Erase Board on Xandra's Door 9:23 p.m.

Hi. Xandra in there?

Know where she went?

■ ■ ■

From: jjacobsen@citycollege.edu
To: aflash@citycollege.edu
Sent: Today 9:28 p.m.
Subject: study break?

X,

Are you out there? In the library? Or getting a late-night snack?

J

■ ■ ■

Dry-Erase Board on Xandra's Door 10:02 p.m.

What time did she leave?

You know when she'll be back?

Sorry. I thought maybe you told each other stuff like that.

■ ■ ■

Dry-Erase Board on Xandra's Door 10:41 p.m.

Still not?

Sorry.

■ ■ ■

Dry-Erase Board on Roger and Paul's Door 11:03 p.m.

You seen Xandra?

Like at all tonight?

Nothing. Just wondering.

■ ■ ■

Dry-Erase Board on Xandra's Door 11:27 p.m.

No?

OK. I'll stop bothering you.

■ ■ ■

From: jjacobsen@citycollege.edu
To: aflash@citycollege.edu
Sent: Today 12:03 a.m.
Subject: Earth to Xandra

Hey—

If you're reading this, please respond. Even if it's to tell me to leave you alone.

J

■ ■ ■

Dry-Erase Board on Jake's Door 12:33 a.m.

What's up? Tatiana says you've been coming by like every 1/2 hour.

Just didn't know where you were.

Didn't know we were keeping tabs on each other.

We're not. Just thought you might wanna hang out a little.

Got worried—can usually find you after 10.

I wasn't on campus.

Where'd you go?

Tippy Top Tap.

By yrself?

W/ Lester.

Oh.

The place we went that time.

I know.

You had a blank look. Like you didn't remember.

I do.

You all right?

I'm fine. Just tired.

Sure?

Yeah.

Looked @ me weird.

How?

Spooky stare. Don't know how to read you.

Don't even try. I'm not a book . . . or magazine . . . or catalog . . .

...more like a crossword puzzle.

Which = fun to figure out!

Never-ending par-tay, those x-words.

Never-ending sarcasm, those x-andras.

Only made 1 sarcastic comment.

But you feel like making more, right?

Don't feel like playing right now.

What feel like?

Sleeping.

Then go sleep.

Lunch tomorrow?

OK.

■ ■ ■

Black-and-White-Speckled English Composition Notebook 1:14 a.m.

Professor Swallows,

Normally right now I'd be writing to Miss Me. That will make sense to you once you've read the rest of my nonjournal. I'm not sure why I picked you. Except that I know you're the only person who will ever actually read this notebook. (Unless it somehow falls into the wrong hands.) AND because you said something hilarious in class. Which means I think you might GET me. Plus, it doesn't hurt that you're real. I don't know if you'll ever respond to any of this. But I sure as hell know my other half won't. And I wonder. If you DO hear things like I do, have you had MORE experiences like mine? Like have you had trouble getting over things? Girls? I need to know. Is it ALWAYS like this? Running over + over in your head what you can do to make some girl want you? Even when you KNOW it's pointless?

You seem so together. With your dress shirts + pressed pants.

I just can't believe that you've been through these things. But then again. I didn't think you got the funny.
—Jacob

A long underwear kind of morning.

Pocket-Size Graph-Paper Notepad with Orange Cover 12:16 p.m.

Go save seats. I'll get food. What want?

Any sandwich.

How bout knuckle?

*How bout *you* save seats & *I* get food?*

Brown Recycled Student Center Napkin 12:31 p.m.

So . . .

So.

How's stuff?

Stuff's good.

Sorry if I weirded you out checking up on you last night.

It's okay. Nice to be worried abt.

Other Side of Brown Recycled Student Center Napkin 12:37 p.m.

What thinking?

Nothing.

Don't believe you.

Really.

Yr not usually like this.

What?

All quiet.

Ummm . . . yes I am.

I mean yr normally livelier.

Just don't have anything to say.

Sure you don't? Not mad?

Nope.

Brown Recycled Napkin Smeared with Tomato Seeds 12:46 p.m.

How was the Tippy Top?

Thought so.

What?

That's what's bothering you.

No. Just wondering. Trying to make conversation.

Well, it was fun.

Yeah?

Yeah. Lester's good @ the ppl guessing game.

You played?

Yep. And he took his turns really seriously. Invented whole lives for the ppl. I guess it makes sense. He's a journalist.

Like the ones who say all the crazy stuff on the radio?

Except in print. Magazines & newspapers. Cool stuff. I think it might be what I want to do.

Is he funny?

Great sense of humor.

Not as great as mine, right?

It's different. He's funny. Yr punny.

Which = funny.

Don't be offended. Wasn't trying to compare you. You set that up.

Was kidding.

Oh. Couldn't tell.

You usually can.

Yr just frustrating sometimes, when you think yr being funny.

Sorr-ee. I'll try + be more funny than frustrating.

Uncrumpled Brown Recycled Napkin with Splotches of Salad Dressing 1:10 p.m.

What doing for Thxgiving?

Meeting up w/ my bro in Boston.

What's he doing there?

He's going to BU.

He is? I'm flattered. But where's he going to school?

*Will you *ever* be able to have a normal conversation?*

What's happening to your funny?

What funny?

THE funny.

Don't know what yr talking abt.

Ketchup on Xandra's Forehead 1:14 p.m.

Brown Recycled Napkin with Globs of Ketchup 1:16 p.m.

Not funny.

You've done that to ME before.

On yr glasses. Not skin.

Fresh Napkin from Next Table Over 1:19 p.m.

What's going on w/ you?

Nothing.

I know what you were doing.

What?

Pretending to be me. Saying you don't know what I'm talking abt.

Whatever.

Why doing this?

Not everything has to be a joke, you know.

I thought you liked it.

Mostly. But that was overboard.

■ ■ ■

Pocket-Size Graph-Paper Notepad with Orange Cover 4:09 p.m.

Whoa! Scared me.

Nice try, Cat.

You're gonna have to pounce a little harder if you want an actual WORD to come out.

■ ■ ■

Dry-Erase Board on Xandra's Door 10:01 p.m.

Hey.

She in?

Thanks—I'll try R+P's room.

I promise. I won't keep coming back.

■ ■ ■

Dry-Erase Board on Roger and Paul's Door 10:05 p.m.

Hi Paul.

Hey X—I actually came looking for YOU.

Come out here a min?

Sorry guys. You're just not as pretty as her.

Pocket-Size Graph-Paper Notepad with Orange Cover 10:07 p.m.

Let's do this in my room.

Do what?

Come in!

Pocket-Size Graph-Paper Notepad with Orange Cover 10:10 p.m.

It's not really a big deal. Just wanna apologize.

For...?

Squirting ketchup on you. Was just playing.

Thanks. I'm over it.

Didn't think it'd upset you like that.

Is there more going on here?

No.

Really?

Going on w/what?

Me going on dates, maybe?

Guess I'm just surprised by how much you seem to like this Bat.

*You mean this *man*?*

Sure. If yr calling him by his last name.

He's just fun. I don't know. I miss having someone to smooch. Know what I mean?

Of course. I want that all the time.

So . . . does that mean . . . you've smooched?

Yep.

Why, what do you think of that?

Nothing. It's fine. That's what you do at the end of dates, right?

Right.

So that's all this Bman thing is abt? Making out?

Like...have we gone further?

Don't tell me that. I mean, is he just a fuck buddy?

Jake!

Sorry. I mean . . . is it just about the kissing—
or is there more to it?

There's other things I like abt him, if that's what you mean.

Like . . . ?

How he whispers in my ear/ sings & plays guitar to me over phone before I go to sleep. Then there's just something abt him. The way he's willing to make himself vulnerable.

Huh?

I know we just met...but he's not afraid to say how crazy he is abt me/ how my voice turns him on over the phone / how my eyes remind him of the sky in a thunderstorm.

I can't believe this cheeseball thinks this will get him
in yr pants . . . + anyway . . . they're more like the lake on
an overcast day.

What?

Your eyes.

Never knew you paid such close attention to the color of my eyes.

I've just looked @ them a lot.

Why does it matter to you if someone else sees them a different way?

Doesn't. Just telling you what I thought. And anyway, I'm right.

*It *does* matter to you!*

Does not.

Stop rolling yr eyes @ me.

Yr "thunderstorm" eyes.

I know it must be hard.

How could you tell? My fly open or something?

For real. I know I haven't been hanging out much lately.

None of my biz anyway.

Not if you don't think it is.

It's not. I'm just afraid I'm getting boring.

How so?

Yr not laughing @ my jokes as much.

I'm just not always in the mood.

+ I don't really allow myself to be vulnerable.

But that doesn't make you boring.

What's it make me?

A liar.

The next day. With leafless trees leaning in the wind.

Piano Key Stationery Inside Music Note Envelope in Jake's Mailbox 12:07 p.m.

Dearest Jacob,

I couldn't help but notice the squeamish look on your face this weekend at the diner. I know how this all looks to you. God, it must look awful. Crazy old Mom ran off with the piano tuner. But really it's not that crazy. You have to trust me on this. Jake, I want to be totally, completely honest with you. If you weren't in the picture, I would've left long ago. Things between your father and me haven't *been right for ages. We got married as young kids, because that's what you did back then. Next I got pregnant because that's what you did after you got married. Someday, Jake, you'll understand that we sometimes have to act on our feelings to be happy. Even grownups. Even grownups with children. I'm not trying to make excuses. Of course, there's no excuse. I mean, I wanted for so many many years to get things right with your dad. Night after night of trying to get him to talk to me. But he was always preoccupied with <u>something.</u> The man simply could never relax or have a heart-to-heart conversation. Which in turn made me feel overly tense all the time. We tried therapy, without much improvement. But I'm not sure that a bigger change would make my feelings any different. Because you see, Jake, I hate to have to say this, but the awful truth is, I'm just not in love with your father. Maybe I never was. I don't know. Maybe that's not something you can know when you're twenty years old. Anyway, the main point of this letter is to ask you to please please please not take our separation personally. I know you say that your silence has nothing to do with me or the breakup. But I can't help wondering. You have every right to be angry with me. Hell, I'm angry with myself. I just want you to be aware that the forces behind what's happening were set in motion long before I even met Curtis. I know you don't like broaching uncomfortable subjects, but I think it will be helpful for us to discuss this over Thanksgiving break. Until then, please be good to yourself.*

Love you,
Mom

■ ■ ■

Black-and-White-Speckled English Composition Notebook 1:14 p.m.

Miss Me,
I've been sitting here for like an hour. Imagining what my voice will sound like when I finally talk. I've been moving my tongue around, making little noises with the back of my throat—trying to

get my vocal cords ready so that it doesn't sound totally weird when words come out. Like when you just wake up or something.

Strange thing is, I feel like I DID just suddenly wake up. From a month-long nap. Like I've been having a terrible dream. And the only way to end the nightmare is to say something. Snap myself out of it.

It HAS to happen. Soon.

—Mr. You

P.S. Sorry it's been so long. And that I wrote to Steven Swallows instead of you last time. Please understand. I'm not trading you in for him. It's just. He's real + you're not.

■ ■ ■

Dry-Erase Board on Jake's Door 1:32 p.m.

Bye.

Leaving already?

Want to be early for my flight.

What?

What, what?

Looked like you wanted to talk. Took deep breath...like before saying something.

No. Just bye. Have fun being you.

?

@ BU

A blustery Thanksgiving Day.

Jake's Finger on Condensation on Curtis's Frosted Beer Mug 5:04 p.m.

HELLO

Jake's Finger on Condensation on His Mom's Glass of White Wine 5:05 p.m.

HI

Blue Ballpoint Pen on Styrofoam Gravy Container 5:12 p.m.

pass potatoes, pls?

Blue Ballpoint Pen on Styrofoam Mashed Potatoes Container 5:14 p.m.

thx

Napkin with Gobble Gobble Catering Logo Slid Across Table 5:18 p.m.

Surprisingly good. But not like when you make everything.

Another Napkin with Gobble Gobble Catering Logo Pushed Across Table 5:19 p.m.

Wasn't a criticism.

Cardboard Top of Aluminum Stuffing Container 5:29 p.m.

Don't know yet.

Yeah, I'm good at math. But it's not so interesting to me.

Nothing really yet.

Someone should just pick a subject out of a hat for me.

Cardboard Top of Stuffing Container Pushed Across Table 5:35 p.m.

Don't tell him that!

■ ■ ■

Pocket-Size Graph-Paper Notepad with Orange Cover 8:31 p.m.

It has nothing to do with this. How many times do I have to tell you?

Just wish you hadn't told him about my math SATs.

mute ≠ not happy

Just that time he called + had me push buttons.

Guess I'll spend Xmas with him. Come here after.

Really. It doesn't bother me. Yes, it's weird + I miss home-cooked turkey. But I'm just into being quiet right now.

Not a chance.

Glad it worked for you. But maybe not talking = my version of therapy.

■ ■ ■

Black-and-White-Speckled English Composition Notebook 10:14 p.m.

Miss Me,
Wow... Curtis. I have to believe that you wouldn't like him either. Maybe you'd pretend to, though. And that would be OK. Cause I know that's what I SHOULD do. I just can't stand that BOOMING voice. His grand way of asking questions: AND WHAT DO YOU EXPECT YOU'LL CHOOSE AS YOUR MAJOR, JACOB? Like it's the title of some opera. I get the feeling he enjoys hearing himself

asking questions more than getting answers. The way he cut in before I was done writing with: DID YOU KNOW I WAS A VOICE MAJOR? Duh. What else could he be?

Maybe that's why Mom + Curtis like each other. He asks the questions + doesn't care about answers/she answers the questions + doesn't care what was asked. Makes for some good self-centered conversation. I wonder if that's what bugs Mom so much about me not talking—she just doesn't understand the urge to keep quiet.

Actually, I'm still really wanting to say something. Desperately. But there's no way in hell it's gonna be cause Mom thinks it'd be "therapeutic." I can't wait to get back to school. To speak when the timing is good. And the words feel just right.
—Mr. You

A still, icy night after a long weekend.

Yellow Legal Paper Chopped Up with Scissors and Dumped into Wastebasket 9:19 p.m.

How to start:
~~I've been wanting to~~
~~There's something I have to~~
~~How was your turkey?~~
~~Hey!~~
~~Look at me! I'm talking!~~
~~These are my first words. They're for you~~

■ ■ ■

Dry-Erase Board on Xandra's Door 10:03 p.m.

X,

Welcome back from BU. (Who B you now if not U?)

Stop by when yr home. Got a surprise.

—J

■ ■ ■

From: aflash@citycollege.edu
To: jjacobsen@citycollege.edu
Sent: Today 11:49 p.m.
Subject: stranded

j,

this city is encased in ice. pretty cool. haha. all the trees, cars, bikes, everything. covered in a layer at least an inch thick. anyway, the airport people didn't think it'd be a good idea for anyone to take off in an ice-encrusted plane. looks like i won't get back to school till tomorrow at the earliest. maybe not even till tues morning.

just wanted to let you know... don't want you *worrying*.

hope you had a happy turkey day.

~x~

■ ■ ■

From: jjacobsen@citycollege.edu
To: aflash@citycollege.edu
Sent: Today 11:58 p.m.
Subject: RE: stranded

X,

Thanks for telling me. That sounds crazy. Wish I could be there, sliding around the ice city with you. Or that you were back here already. I'm going through Xandra withdrawal! Give me my fix!

J

A deceptively sunny Tuesday.

Margin of Jake's Jazz Notes 2:31 p.m.

I'm gonna do RE-SCHLONG-ULOUSLY badly on this exam next week. Don't even remember what bebop means.

Margin of Paul's Jazz Notes 2:32 p.m.

Maybe you should cunsult a COCK-TIONERY.

Margin of Jake's Jazz Notes 2:32 p.m.

Maybe YOU should!

Margin of Paul's Jazz Notes 2:34 p.m.

Don't be such a COCK-TATOR.

Margin of Roger's Jazz Notes 2:35 p.m.

Stop with the cock jokes! My hose might go slosh!

Margin of Paul's Jazz Notes 2:36 p.m.

I thought that was Jakes hose. For Xandra.

Margin of Jake's Jazz Notes 2:38 p.m.

Why do you have to be so PRE-COCK-TABLE?

■ ■ ■

Dry-Erase Board on Jake's Door 4:02 p.m.

Hey—you moving back in?

Oh. Yeah. Guess you'd need that.

Have good break?

I had to spend mine with Mom + Curtis.

What's going on in your life these days?

Yeah. Sucks how early it gets dark.

And it's not even officially winter yet.

■ ■ ■

Dry-Erase Board on Jake's Door 5:23 p.m.

Hi!

Yr back! When get in, Icegirl?

Round noon. Then straight to classes. I'm beat. Up @ 5 am.

Come IN already!

Pocket-Size Graph-Paper Notepad with Orange Cover 5:27 p.m.

How was trip?

Fun. Went to Mapporium—like walking through inside of globe. You?

Lame. Hung out w/ Mom + Curtis.

Why lame?

Mom trying to talk me into talking. Her playing piano w/ him singing... sickening.

Yuck.

Hey, wanna go on an odd outing this weekend? I'll pick place.

Would. Except told Lester I'd go ice skating w/ him...
@ that free outdoor rink downtown.

Yr still talking to that guy?

Yep.

While away?

Free cell mins on weekend.

Didn't call me . . .

b/c yr not talking.

I know. Was kidding.

When going skating?

Saturday.

How bout we do something Sun?

Got paper due Mon. Will need that day to write. Lots of hw to catch up on this week.

Fri?

Going out w/ Tatiana for her b-day.

Why don't you come ice skating on Sat?

I'm no good.

I'll help.

Lemme think abt it.

Come on. It'll be fun. You guys should meet.

OK. But only if you don't laugh @ my skating.

Deal.

*What thinking? Looked like you were gonna *say* something. Like last time.*

What time?

Don't do this.

Do what?

Uggghl

OK, OK—just playing—fun to get you all riled up!

Ouch, Punchy! Won't give in to you if you keep punching! You meant that time right when you were leaving? How it looked like I was gonna talk?

Yes!

~~I wasn't gonna say anyth~~

It's just. This is nice. Sitting on my bed w/ you. That's all.

I miss the way things were BB.

BB?

Before Batman.

You mean BL?

If you insist.

Things are different now. But only a little.

Yr just moving so quickly. Don't wanna see you get hurt.

That *all* yr worried about?

Yeah. That + he's so much older than us.

Only 5 years.

But he could take advantage of you.

I'm a big girl.

Yr actually pretty small. But what I mean is . . . sometimes you can't see what yr getting yrself into . . . b/c yr too involved to step back + look.

You did it again.

What?

Opened yr mouth. Must have something big on yr mind.

Yr so persistent. Don't you know nobody likes to say what they're REALLY thinking?

It can be tough. But sometimes it helps. And anyway, does this mean I'm right? You *do* have more on yr mind?

OK. Yes. Yr right.

Maybe it'd make you feel better to say it.

Or maybe it'd make YOU feel better to hear it. Think mstly it's >

imp for ppl to HEAR what some1 thnks than prsn to SAY it. What's pt of telling, when clrly KNOW what's on mnd?

...huh?

You know what it says.

Don't.

Playing dumb?

No!

Then I'll spell it out (literally): I think mostly it's more important for people to HEAR what someone else is thinking than for that person to SAY it. What's the point of telling you things anyway, when you clearly KNOW what's on my mind?

Yr such a pain in the ass, you know? Why don't you just say what yr thinking if I know what it is?

b/c... what if you don't?

■ ■ ■

Page Ripped From Black-and-White-Speckled English Composition Notebook and Thrown into Wastebasket 12:22 a.m.

Miss Me,

Aaaaaaagh! It didn't work. I don't know what's wrong with me. I just couldn't DO it! But it's like, how CAN I do it when...

I'm chasing after X + she's chasing after someone else?
if...
I keep quiet → X will never know that I want her +
we'll avoid awkwardness
avoiding awkwardness = keeping her as a friend

keeping her as a friend = not screwing up by saying
the wrong thing
saying the wrong thing = what happened with Sean
what happened with Sean = no more friend
so doesn't...
not screwing things up = keeping quiet?

Man. I can't believe I'm actually looking for answers from you. If you ARE out there, I'm sorry. I have to stop. Or I'll really believe I'm going to hear back. What is WRONG with me? Why can't I just let things go? Not let them bother me. Like a normal

JAKE—
STOP WRITING TO A FIGMENT OF YOUR IMAGINATION!

■ ■ ■

Black-and-White-Speckled English Composition Notebook 12:44 a.m.

Professor Swallows,
I think maybe I'm going crazy. You'll see that I ripped out the page before this. Because I started actually believing that Miss Me existed.

I've been all in my head since I stopped talking. Which has been good in a lot of ways. But maybe it's starting to get to me. YOU don't even know that I'm not talking. But I'm sure you will by the time you read this.

This whole punning thing is getting annoying too. I wish I could just hear things the right way the 1st time. Like this morning when the radio announcer said, "Ten soldiers have been wounded. Six of them seriously." I honestly thought she meant they were joking about the 1st 4. As in: but seriously, folks, only 6 were wounded. You believed there were 10? Fooled you! But of course that's not what she meant. And when she was talking about the pledge drive, saying, "We need your support now. That's right. NOW. And to give you extra incentive, as if our programming wasn't enough, we're going to do a drawing. For a bicycle!" All I could think was, "What would a BICYCLE do with a DRAWING? Hang it on its spokes?" It took me at least a minute to hear it the right way. S.e.r.i.o.u.s.l.y.

Anyway. I'm not sure why writing to you is any better than Miss Me, seeing as I won't hand this in till the course is over. Speaking of your course. I've got to figure out what the hell to write about for my paper. And what to do about reading it to the class. I hope you don't think I'm just a mega pain in your ass.

—Jacob

That weekend. Warm enough that it doesn't hurt to be outside.

Pocket-Size Graph-Paper Notepad with Orange Cover 1:06 p.m.

Hi.

Nice to meet you too.

I guess she told you. I'm not such a good skater.

That's OK. I can get them myself.

Wow, you've got your own?

Small Piece of Graph Paper Waved in Air 1:13 p.m.

10½

Back of Small Piece of Graph Paper Left on Counter Beside a Row of Ice Skates 1:15 p.m.

Thanks.

Pocket-Size Graph-Paper Notepad with Orange Cover 1:19 p.m.

Oh, it's been OK.

Yeah, sometimes it's frustrating. But I also like keeping quiet. X makes it a lot easier. With her I don't even feel like I'm not talking. Most of the time.

Jake, Xandra, and Lester's Skate Blades on Ice 1:27 p.m.

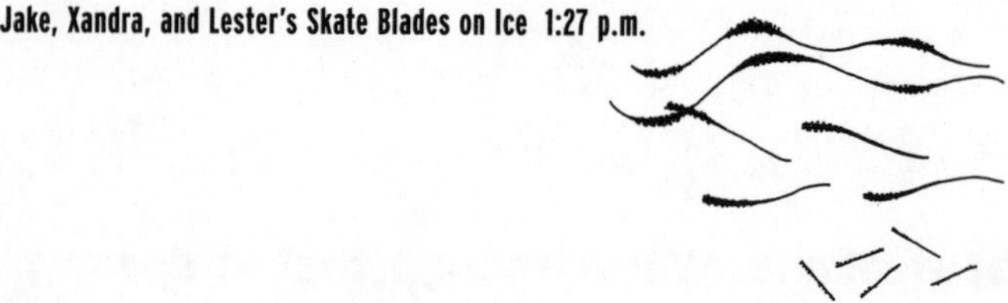

Pocket-Size Graph-Paper Notepad with Orange Cover Leaned Against Side of Skating Rink 1:40 p.m.

Ankles hurt.

Have to keep yr legs straighter. Go to bench. I'll tighten yr laces.

Pocket-Size Graph-Paper Notepad with Orange Cover 1:44 p.m.

Thanks.

Lester's good @ this.

Grew up near a pond. Learned to skate w/o railings.

Maybe he could teach somthng to those ppl who keep grabbng me when falling. Makes me go down too. Guess I don't know how to warn ppl when I crash either.

Would be easier if you were talking.

Well I'm not.

Hey there, Mr. Defensive. Just an observation.

Ready to go back out?

+ get run over by some 5-yr-old hockey champ? Sure.

Grab my arm.

Jake and Xandra's Skate Blades on Ice 1:56 p.m.

Lester's Skate Blades on Ice 1:58 p.m.

Jake and Xandra's Skate Blades on Ice 2:12 p.m.

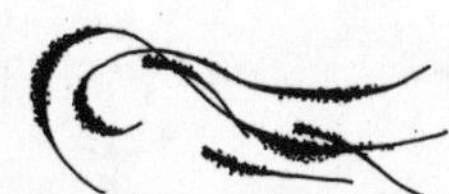

Pocket-Size Graph-Paper Notepad with Orange Cover 2:15 p.m.

Someone's gotten more comfortable on ice! Don't you know checking's not allowed?

Someone's lucky I'm not even better, or by end of day she'd = Iceface Flash.

Let's go show Lester yr new skills.
I think he saw them when lapped us like 5,000x.
I'm gonna try going backwards.

Jake, Xandra, and Lester's Skate Blades on Ice 2:19 p.m.

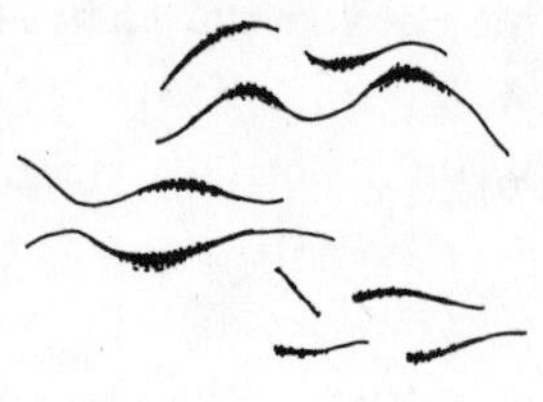

Side of Paper Hot Chocolate Cup at Skating Rink 2:48 p.m.

Lester wants to go → movie after this.
Sounds good. Which one?
The Man Who Laughs.
Haven't heard of it.
Silent film w/ live orchestra. Abt guy w/permanent smile.
Cool!

Pocket-Size Graph-Paper Notepad with Orange Cover 2:56 p.m.

So does anyone ever call you Batman?

Did she tell you it was my idea to call?

I would've done it. If I were talking.

I wonder if we would've wound up being friends 1st. If I'd been the one to call.

Yeah, I guess you can never really know.
But here's something funny: I used to think I was Batman.
Ran around in Underoos + a mask. To me it wasn't pretending.
It was Jake = Batman.

Really? You didn't even have a mask?

Fraud!

Pocket-Size Graph-Paper Notepad with Orange Cover 3:15 p.m.

I've been thinking, maybe it's not such a good idea for you to go → movie.

No?

No.

I'll be good.

Was just trying to relate to him—w/ all the Batman stuff.

It's not just that.

I think he wants us to be alone. It's our 1st movie together & everything.

Could be really romantic.

I won't go then.

My life = a silent film anyway.

Don't need to see it in a movie.

Sure yr not hurt?

Don't worry. I'm tough.

I won't let Batman get to me. I'm the Joker.

That's exactly what you are.

Jake's Finger in Dirt on Lester's Car 3:33 p.m.

BYE

■ ■ ■

Ripped Piece of Graph Paper Pressed Against Window Between Front and Back Seat of Cab, Emphasized with Knocking 3:38 p.m.

City College please.

Ripped Piece of Graph Paper Passed Through Hole in Window Between Front and Back Seat of Cab with Fifteen Dollars 4:01 p.m.

Thanks . . . keep the change.

■ ■ ■

Yellow Legal Paper Burned with Cigarette Lighter, Then Flushed Down Men's Room Toilet in Jake's Dorm 6:06 p.m.

Xandra,

I'm not sure if you saw it while you were waving at me from the Batmobeetle. I really hope you didn't. Not because I think it's wrong for boys to cry.

but . . .
if you saw me crying → you'd know how I feel about you

and . . .
now that you have a boyfriend →
you SHOULDN'T know how I feel about you

I wished today a few times that I could've just blurted it all out. How I want you. And he doesn't deserve you. Because you've known ME longer. And we get each other more. Except I realized that would seem immature + unattractive + wouldn't get me anywhere.

but . . .
someday you'll probably break up with Batman →
things will be back to normal

I hope that happens soon,
Jake

P.S. I have no idea why I wrote this. When I knew from the start where it'd end up.

■ ■ ■

Dry-Erase Marker Pressed Very Lightly on Xandra's Dry-Erase Board 1:02 a.m.

What're you guys listening to?

Put ear on door.

Is it what we think it is?

I think so.

No—I know so.

She's a screamer!

& moaner

mostly screamer

Where you going? Not enjoying the show?

It's nasty to hear your friends doing it. I wouldn't want to hear you 2 either.

Its not like that between me and Roger.

You know what I mean.

Completely Erased Dry-Erase Board on Xandra's Door 1:10 a.m.

I'm going to bed.

■ ■ ■

Yellow Legal Paper Folded in Eighths and Stuffed into Ripped-Open Self-Stick Security Envelope 1:25 a.m.

Xandra,

Right now you are getting batfucked. And guess what. You're a screamer. There's a huddle of smirking guys standing by your door. I don't know which would make me feel better:

to tell you tomorrow and watch you squirm

\- or -

not tell you and let you hear it from someone else

It just seems so real now. I can actually picture you in there. All naked. And even though I don't want to . . . because I bet his tiny-little-stupid-ass is all hairy. . . I can picture HIM too. And I wish that what I heard coming from you were unhappy noises. Because then I'd break down the door and kick his Liddle-Bhutt. But. (Butt?) You are definitely NOT unhappy. So I will stay where I am. Unable to sleep.

—Jake

Slightly warmer the next day, with tops of buildings fading into fog.

Dry-Erase Board on Jake's Door 5:37 p.m.

Why was Paulger making monkey noises @ me?

You don't wanna know.

I asked, didn't I?

You sure they were MONKEY noises?

*If not, then it sounded like they *really* liked me.*

They REALLY liked listening to you last night.

*You could *hear*?*

Whole floor could.

Dry-Erase Board on Roger and Paul's Door 5:45 p.m.

At least I'm getting some.

Pocket-Size Graph-Paper Notepad with Orange Cover 5:47 p.m.

Don't be too mad at them. You WERE pretty loud. And really, I think you made them happy.

It's just embarrassing. And not like I want to be fantasy material for them.

Yr all red.

Thanks for pointing it out.

Shouldn't let em get to you too much.

I'm not.

Then why so 

Don't wanna talk abt it.

See? You DO understand.

*It's not that I don't want to talk abt it. I don't want to talk abt it w/ *you*.*

Sounds juicy.

Fuck off.

It's easier to fuck ON. You should know that.

~~Hey, I didn't mean~~ Please. No tears. I'm sorry.

Here. Punch me. Hard as you can.

Again. Harder.

That's all you've got?

OK! Enough!

You hungry? Lemme take you out for dinner.

White Paper Tablecloth at Burger Palace 6:02 p.m.

So what's going on? I promise. No jokes.

I don't know, Jake. It has to do w/ you. Let's talk abt something else.

Aren't you the one who said it's better to say what you have to say?

Yeah...& that's true. But it's gonna make you feel bad.

We'll be even. I made you feel pretty bad today already.

Good pt. Okay then. Where to begin? It's been going on for a while now. But yesterday it started when I told Lester I felt bad abt disinviting you from the movie. You seemed really hurt...& he accused me of having feelings for you.

What'd you say?

That you & I are really close, but it's not like that.

+ he didn't believe you?

He just doesn't like how we are together. Writing notes all the time. He says it's like we have a secret language.

Not so secret. Anyone can write notes.

But you have to admit, the way you do it w/ me is different than w/ anyone else. Passing notebook back & forth/ little abbreviations & stuff...our own language.

True.

& then there's the fighting. He doesn't like how we push each other around. On our 2nd date he saw my bruises. At 1st he thought I was being abused. But when I explained it, he said it was just as bad.

Why?

b/c that meant we were flirting.

Should we stop acting that way?

*I don't want to. That's part of why our friendship is so much fun. But I feel like I *have to* stop if I want to keep dating him.*

Why?

I think he'd get so jealous he'd dump me.

I know you really like him, but would that be SO terrible?

Aside from this, everything's great w/ him. And also...

I can't deal w/ another rejection.

What're you talking about? How many other rejections are there?

3

Name them.

James: my high school boyfriend who said we needed to see other ppl when we went to college. Kevin: this sophomore who I totally wanted the first few weeks of school & it seemed like he wanted me too. Except then it turned out it wasn't like that for him.

That's 2.

Yeah.

You said there were 3.

Don't worry abt it.

Ketchup on Xandra's Cheeseburger 6:20 p.m.

Dry-Erase Board on Xandra's Door 7:05 p.m.

I want dessert.

Me too.

Having another pudding craving.

*Sounds *so* good right now.*

I think I still have a box in my room.

Get it!

Dry-Erase Board on Jake's Door 7:11 p.m.

One problem: we need milk.

Someone's gotta have milk in dorm fridge.

Brilliant.

Small Piece of Graph Paper Nestled in Milk Carton Handle 7:14 p.m.

To the person who bought this milk:

I will buy you a new one.

Pocket-Size Graph-Paper Notepad with Orange Cover 7:22 p.m.

Got a spoon?

Jake's Hand in Instant Pudding Mix and Milk 7:23 p.m.

Pocket-Size Graph-Paper Notepad with Orange Cover 7:24 p.m.

Jake! I have a spoon in my room!

Jake's Pudding-Covered Hand on Xandra's Hand 7:24 p.m.

Xandra's Pudding-Covered Hand on Jake's Face 7:25 p.m.

Pudding on Floor That Oozed Out of Jake and Xandra's Clasped Hands 7:26 p.m.

Pudding on Wall That Just Missed Jake's Ear 7:27 p.m.

Pudding Shampooed into Xandra's Hair 7:28 p.m.

Pudding Oozing Down Jake and Xandra's Arms from Between Their Entwined Fingers 7:31 p.m.

Pudding from Jake's Fingers on Wall 7:34 p.m.

EAT THE REST

Pudding from Xandra's Fingers on Wall 7:36 p.m.

IT'S YRS

Pudding from Jake's Fingers on Wall 7:37 p.m.

SHARE

Pudding from Xandra's Fingers on Wall 7:43 p.m.

NEED MOP

Pudding from Jake's Fingers on Wall 7:43 p.m.

\+ SHOWERS

■ ■ ■

Dry-Erase Board on Jake's Door 7:56 p.m.

What happened in their? Diarea fight?

■ ■ ■

Pocket-Size Graph-Paper Notepad with Orange Cover 8:45 p.m.

So can we not do things like that anymore?

He'd prefer it.

But what do YOU want?

I want to. But no bruises.

That'll be difficult . . . but if that's how it's gotta be.

Hey. What were you thinking before? When you gave me that intense look?

What look?

Stop. I know you know what I'm talking abt.

Just tell me so I'm sure.

When you had me pinned to the wall.

Dunno . . . deciding whether or not to lick a glob of pudding off yr forehead.

Why didn't you?

Thought was time to stop . . . + eat pudding already. And holy shit, I just remembered I have a paper due tomorrow.

■ ■ ■

Yellow Legal Paper Folded in Eighths and Squeezed into Ripped-Open Self-Stick Security Envelope 9:00 p.m.

Xandy,

I can tell. You're about to get fed up with me + my roundabout ways. I want to make sure that doesn't happen. I know that means answering all the questions you have about me. I just have to do it on my own terms.

when you pester me → I want to do it less
because then . . .
there's all this pressure to say what you want to hear +
I'm never sure what that is

But I REALLY want to do something to change things. Make you feel like I'm trying.

it's just . . .
(I want to answer your questions – revealing too much) +
I don't know if that = possible
maybe . . .
if I set up a question-answering session → it'll be on my terms

I just hope you don't ask anything too big too quick. I might freeze again.
—Jake

■ ■ ■

From: jjacobsen@citycollege.edu
To: sswallows@citycollege.edu
Sent: Today 9:34 p.m.
Subject: favor

Professor Swallows,

It's Jacob Jacobsen. From English 1. I'm writing with a strange request.

You might be wondering why I never say anything in class. At first it was because I didn't think I had anything to say. Now I'm still not sure I have anything to say, but I'm also not saying anything. What I mean is, I haven't been talking for about a month. I'm supposed to read my paper on Monday, which as you know is the last day of class. I have a feeling I still won't be talking by then. So I'm wondering, would you be willing to read my paper for me?

Thank you for considering this.

Sincerely,
Jacob Jacobsen

In the morning. Cold, motionless branches look like staticky hair reaching for the sky.

From: sswallows@citycollege.edu
To: jjacobsen@citycollege.edu
Sent: Today 7:16 a.m.
Subject: RE: favor

Jacob,

I've noticed you scribbling madly at your desk during freewrites and critiques. But I never guessed that you'd taken the path of elective mutism. I can't help but wonder…why? I'm not sure if you've looked through all of the information in that big blue folder they gave you the first day of school (I probably wouldn't either)—but if you take a look in there, you'll find information on the various support services that the school has to offer.

Re: your paper, I'd be happy to read it if you're still not talking. Though I do think this is an issue you should work out eventually. And sooner rather than later. Feel free to talk to me (or somehow let me know) if you're unsure of where to look for help.

Also—you can call me Steven, like I said on the first day of class.

Steven Swallows

■ ■ ■

Jake's Computer Screen 8:19 a.m.

Your computer has unexpectedly shut down.
Unsaved files may have been lost.

reason: unknown

■ ■ ■

From: jjacobsen@citycollege.edu
To: sswallows@citycollege.edu
Sent: Today 8:25 a.m.
Subject: uh-oh

Steven,

Thank you for your concern. I think I'll be OK without the stuff in the blue folder. (You're right, I haven't read most of it.) Thanks also for agreeing to read my paper. But now I have a bigger problem. This is so embarrassing, because I know I should've been saving as I wrote. But you see, I was up all night finishing the paper. It's not like I just started writing last night... OK, I won't lie. I started last night. I just didn't know what to write about. Unlike everyone else in the class, I'm not into sharing my deepest darkest secrets. And it took a lot for me to write what I wrote about—which is this situation with my friend. Really, a couple different friends. How everything's falling apart. Well, I changed the names and everything so people wouldn't know who it was. I hope that's OK. What am I talking about? It doesn't even matter because what happened is, my computer crashed. I'd gotten so into what I was writing that I didn't think about saving. And there you have it. No paper. I feel terrible. Not only because I think I'll fail, but because I really sort of liked what I was writing. Is there any way I can have an extension? Thanks for your understanding. If you give it to me... and even if you don't.

Jacob Jacobsen

From: sswallows@citycollege.edu
To: jjacobsen@citycollege.edu
Sent: Today 9:10 a.m.
Subject: RE: uh-oh

Jacob,

This is a tricky one. As you know, I rarely grant extensions. You're right. You should've saved your work. I don't, however, wish to see you fail. Because as you also know, failure in this course means you have to take it over again next semester. I have to be honest: your work has been consistently disappointing in this class. Disappointing because I think you're a much better writer than what you've demonstrated in your work. You are a consistently great observer. Your mind makes interesting connections—and that's clear in your papers. You also often have a look of intense concentration when we're doing class critiques, which indicates to me that there's a lot going on up there. But when it comes to reflecting on observations in your essays, you give me nothing. Everything remains on the surface. This is incredibly frustrating, because it leaves your reader (namely, me) with an empty feeling. You've built up these interesting ideas . . . and then left me hanging. As a result, your average is on the cusp of a C and a B. Failing on this paper would put your average below a C, which is the equivalent of failing.

Stick around after class today. We'll talk. Or at least try to find a fair solution.

Until then,
Steven

■ ■ ■

Brown Recycled Napkin with Tiny Rips All Over Bottom Edge 12:12 p.m.

You look awful.

Thanks.

No, really. You okay?

Didn't sleep. Stayed up writing a paper that my computer destroyed anyway.

Sucks! What was it about?

Don't remember.

Cause it was soooooo long ago, huh?

Just don't wanna get into it. Sick of thinking abt it.

That's fair.

Hey. I came up w/ an idea. Of what to do w/ all yr questions.

What questions?

The ones I won't answer.

What's the plan?

We'll have Direct Questions Night. Tonight. I'll host it. In my room. Only 1 person will be invited: you.

What'll we do on DQN?

Duh. You'll ask me direct questions.

Will I get direct answers?

Didn't say that.

Why so afraid of directness?

If you asked me direct Qs they'd all be abt what I was thinking some time when I said something + we were doing this or that...

Yeah, but they'd all be pointing to something larger.

What'd that be? Can you think of a larger direct Q for me?

Yes.

What?

Not now.

You know. Yr in control now. But. If you asked me → I'd be in control b/c I wouldn't have to answer + you'd want to know the answer.

You make it so much more complicated than it has to be. Stop grinning.

■ ■ ■

Chalkboard in Jake's English Classroom 2:10 p.m.

Sorry. Computer crashed.

Lost my voice screaming at a concert.

■ ■ ■

Pocket-Size Graph-Paper Notepad with Orange Cover 3:37 p.m.

You still want me to stay?

Yeah. I write notes.

Chalkboard in Jake's English Classroom 3:38 p.m.

Then so will I.

Why don't we go to my office?

White Pad with Steven Swallows's Name on Top 3:43 p.m.

I want to start with this "not having anything to say" business.

What about it?

Explain what you mean.

I don't know. I just listen to the papers in class.

And I have no response.

I don't believe you.

It's true.

Then what's all the scribbling about? It doesn't look like unengaged doodling.

It's not nice—the stuff I think about other people's essays.

It doesn't have to be. That's why we have critiques.

I know.

And I also know you're trying to get us to say what we really think. Give honest opinions. But I'm afraid I'll upset someone.

There are ways of saying things without upsetting people.

If you say it constructively and they're still upset, then they don't understand that your opinion is valid and that your comments are meant to be helpful.

Why does it matter to you if I give comments or not?

Because from what I've seen, you have insightful comments.

Not the usual "I liked it."

What's so funny?

Something on the radio next door. The news just cracks me up sometimes.

What did you hear?

You might think this is really weird. But they were talking about putting an acting principal in a school. And I was thinking like the new principal's gonna go in and put on a one-man show. Do monologues all the time.

Or perhaps this school could use a singing and dancing principal?

You DO get it! I thought maybe you did.

What do you mean?

I have this habit of hearing things literally. Lately I haven't been able to stop. There was something you said the other day that I heard that way. It was pretty dirty, though.

I saw that funny look. I figured it was the double entendre.

And yes, I like wordplay too. Because I like words. Which brings me to the other part of what I wanted to say to you. And that is, you remind me a lot of myself when I was your age.

How?

Frustrated over slow-moving classes. People putting politeness over quality. I see you rolling your eyes when students are overly complimentary. Am I right?

Pretty much. In your class, at least.

Problem is, critiquing gets you nowhere unless you produce respectable work—a lesson I learned the hard way when I was about your age. By thinking I could get away with writing my papers hastily the night before they were due. I knew I was good. Except unlike you, I was vocal about my frustration. My English instructor showed me—through my grades—that I had to put my money where my mouth was.

Are you saying I don't?

I'm saying you have interesting observations. About what's happening around you and about other people's writing. You must be learning a lot from your silence these days . . . whether you need help from the "blue folder" or not. I think you have it in you to write a good paper. That's why I've decided to give you until the week after finals to turn in your paper. To prove to me that you can do it. This time you'll have no excuses.

What do you want me to do that I haven't been doing?

You're great at describing the whats. But I want to know the <u>hows</u>. And the <u>whys</u>. Be reflective. Write about <u>how</u> you feel about the whats and <u>why</u> you feel that way. Complete the picture.

I'll try. Thanks. A lot.

■ ■ ■

Brown Recycled Student Center Napkin with Ice Cream Drips 6:32 p.m.

Isn't this ice cream good, Roger?

Yes, Paul, it is. Yum.

Why are you guys being so weird?

Brown Recycled Napkin with Ice Cream Drips Flipped Over Quickly 6:32 p.m.

Hi Jenni.

Hey there, Jenni.

Look at U guys all writing notes. 2 cute!

Want 2 sit with us?

I would. But got 2 run 2 a meeting.

Not even time 4 dessert?

I don't eat dessert.

2 bad. I never 8 ice cream this good!

I bet. But don't want 2 get fat.

This is a fun game. Jake, U R 2 cool.

Thanks. But it's not really a game.

Well, whatever it is. Anywho, gotta run, B4 I'm 2 late! C U layta!

Another Brown Recycled Napkin with Ice Cream Drips 6:39 p.m.

Don't get it.

What?

Y she thinks your better than us.

She nose I'm more authentic than U 2.

Eye guess.

■ ■ ■

Pocket-Size Graph-Paper Notepad with Orange Cover 8:11 p.m.

Ready... set... DIRECT QUESTIONS NIGHT... Go!

Yes? Alexandra Flash. You're up first.

Jacob Jacobsen. My first question for you is: Do you trust me?

Well, Alexandra. To be honest, there are only 2 ppl I've trusted completely. And. I've hurt them both.

How are you defining trust?

Trust = telling someone about the things that make you sleepless. Or trying to, at least. Wanting to.

I like that way of putting it.

When you have that understanding w/ someone, you want to hold on to them . . . + if they slip away, you feel like you did something terribly wrong.

Are you ready for question #2?

Hit me.

Ouch! Not so hard! Remember? No bruising.

*No bruising *me*.*

Q 2: How have you hurt those ppl?

1 of them I slept w/ a few of his girlfriends . . . + the other . . . I'm not telling.

Why not?

That's a 3rd question, but I'll answer it anyway. Cause I know I've hurt this person, but I don't know if I've lost them yet. I'm afraid I will.

That's really sad.

I know. It's REALLY sad.

*I'm *serious*. Don't mock me.*

I'm not. I know it's S

A

D.

But it's not a direct answer.

I know.

Can I get one?
No.
But this is DQN!
I know. I thought I'd be able to do this. But I just can't.
Why not?
I might lose that person faster.
*Will you *ever* answer me directly?*
Maybe if we play again sometime. Got to study more for physics final.
I guess you could call this Direct Questions Night. But Indirect Answers Night is more like it.

■ ■ ■

Yellow Legal Paper Folded in Eighths and Pushed Between Other Folded Yellow Legal Papers in Ripped-Open Self-Stick Security Envelope 12:33 a.m.

Xandy,
Trust me. I REALLY wanted to do it tonight. Tell you everything. Tell you OUT LOUD. About how I wish I'd kissed you during the pudding fight + that night you spent in my bed + all the times we've wrestled on my floor.

but...
having you close + thinking how my answers might
make you distant = too much for me to handle
+ I can never think of the RIGHT way to say any of this

while we're together, every scenario I imagine =
scaring you off

I hope you understand. I'm doing this so we can keep what we have.
—Jake

P. S. But I know. If I don't do something with the things in my head, something bad will happen. I don't know what. But right now I think I could punch the wall by my bed and make it all the way through.

The following evening. With a sharp sliver of a moon.

Dry-Erase Board on Xandra's Door 10:58 p.m.

Looks like what you drew on my cheeseburger.

Dunno what yr talking about.

You do.

Don't remember drawing anything.

Right. You know what I'm talking about. In Burger Palace.

?

Yr impossible.

Bad memory.

Fuck, Jake. That's gonna bruise. Why'd you have to punch me?

Freshly Erased Dry-Erase Board on Xandra's Door 11:05 p.m.

1.
2. I can't tell you #1.
3. So I hit you.
4. Lots of things about me are this way.

What's #1?

You know.

Don't.

Yeah. You do. But you need me to write it?

Yes.

Already told you.

Don't know what yr talking abt.

WHO's impossible?

Just write it.

1. The ketchup
2. I can't tell you #1.
3. So I hit you.
4. Lots of things about me are this way.

That tells me nothing.

<u>on the cheeseburger:</u>

1. The ketchup I don't remember (see #2)
2. I can't tell you #1.
3. So I hit you.
4. Lots of things about me are this way.

Jesus.

Jake.

You know, having conversations w/ you takes abt 10x as long as they do in real life.
Up yrs. I just told you something you needed to know. I revealed a hell of a lot.
Yr right. You did.

Completely Erased Dry-Erase Board on Xandra's Door 11:18 p.m.

Good night, Xandra.

■ ■ ■

Yellow Legal Paper Folded in Eighths and Crumpled Slightly as Pushed into Ripped-Open Self-Stick Security Envelope 11:27 p.m.

Xandra,
I swear. I didn't even realize I was writing a code with that list. I just left off #1 to be funny. Confuse you a little. Then I wrote ketchup and it all fell into place. I discovered what it all really meant as I was writing it. You have to admit. It was pretty CLEVER.

Except even though I'm feeling proud right now. I'm also kinda nauseous. Because now you know everything. You know it for sure. Before you just THOUGHT you knew it. And now's when the shit's gonna go down. If only I hadn't been so clever tonight, I could've put it off longer. Maybe forever?
—Jake

The next night. Under a starless sky.

Dry-Erase Board on Jake's Door 7:47 p.m.

Why can't you say things straightforwardly?

What mean? Told you things last night. Important things.

Tell me what you told me.

If you don't know, yr not as smart as I thought.

Then I'm an idiot.

What think I meant?

Freshly Erased Dry-Erase Board on Jake's Door 7:51 p.m.

Think I know, but if wrong I'll be embarrassed. Want you to tell me. So frustrating having it in cryptic list form.

Why don't you write me yr own list?

■ ■ ■

Butcher Paper Beside Stolen Sign Collection on Roger's Wall 8:09 p.m.

Your notes aren't any better than mine. We need methods to help remember this stuff.

Charlie Parker SEXtet

Louis Armstrong and his HOT Five!

How 'bout that John Cocktrane?

Or Sonny Ballins?

Herbie Han-schlong.

Don't forget Butty Goodman.

Or my friend Theloniass Monk.

Jake, did I ever tell you your My Punny Valentine?

We are going to ace this!

■ ■ ■

College-Ruled Paper Torn from Spiral-Bound Notebook, Slipped Under Jake's Door 11:10 p.m.

Looking at my love bruises, I think...

1. I feel really close to you.
2. Sometimes that makes me want to kiss you.
3. I don't know how to tell you #2.
4. Cause I'm afraid you won't kiss me back.
5. Or won't be honest about how you feel.
6. So I've given up.

■ ■ ■

Back of College-Ruled Paper Torn from Spiral-Bound Notebook, Slipped Inside Ripped-Open Self-Stick Security Envelope 11:16 p.m.

X,

How could I have let this happen? I feel so stupid.

I just don't know what to do. One thing's for sure. These letters to you are pointless now that you've given

■ ■ ■

Toe of Jake's Boot in Snowy Sand 11:32 p.m.

Singe Marks from Jake's Lighter on Bottom Edge of Ripped-Open Self-Stick Security Envelope 11:34 p.m.

Lighter Fluid from Jake's Lighter Poured on Ripped-Open Self-Stick Security Envelope 11:37 p.m.

Singe Marks on Ripped-Open Self-Stick Security Envelope 11:39 p.m.

Burn Marks on Left Sleeve of Jake's Jacket 11:39 p.m.

Jake's Arm in Snowy Sand 11:40 p.m.

Burnt Bits of Self-Stick Security Envelope and Yellow Legal Papers Skimming Top of Lake 11:43 p.m.

■ ■ ■

Black-and-White-Speckled English Composition Notebook 12:26 a.m.

Steven,

There's this concept we studied in physics. All about how things have "potential energy" when they're sitting still. Especially in high places. When the thing drops or rolls down a hill, the energy becomes more real. They call it "kinetic." Then there's food. To find how much energy it has, you can burn it. This made me start thinking about the objects around me. How they ALL have potential. And to figure out what it is, you'd just have to burn them. Don't worry. I didn't turn into a pyro or anything. Just tried it once with a photograph. It wasn't very satisfying. Plus, it smelled like chemicals. And then tonight. I tried it with a whole bunch of letters I wrote but never sent. To this girl I like in a major way. That wasn't so successful either. Because they didn't burn as quickly or completely as I'd hoped. Anyway. A couple hours ago I wanted more than anything to get rid of those letters. So I did. But you know? I couldn't tell a damn thing once they were burned and gone.

It's only hitting me now. Cause there might be a time that I actually WANT to deliver them to the person they're for. Or I might want to go back and take a look. Remind myself of how I screwed up by NOT delivering the letters. And make sure I never do it again. So this is how I'm discovering it. What it feels like. To have stored up a ton of information. Hoarded it away in an envelope. And then have it go away.

The science books are right about potential. It's easier to lose it than to get it back.

—Jacob

The next day. With clouds like an old man's beard.

Back Cover of Extra Blue Book on Paul's Foldover Desktop in Auditorium 3:49 p.m.

How'd you make out?

Awesome. These blue books sure are good kissers.

Too bad I wound up with paper cuts all over my lips though.

How bout you?

Same. Except my cuts are on my tunge.

You should know not to move so fast with a blue book.

Seriously. How do you think you did?

I think I actually memorized enough to pass.

Me too.

I know. It seemed easy. We didn't even study very schlong.

■ ■ ■

Dry-Erase Board on Jake's Door 10:22 p.m.

You got my list?

Yes.

What think?

I'm not writing this on here . . . come inside.

Pocket-Size Graph-Paper Notepad with Orange Cover 10:25 p.m.

It was shocking.

*Was sposed to be. But what'd you *think*?*

You don't wanna know.

I asked, didn't I?

You've REALLY been wanting to kiss me?

At times.

Me too. Lots of times.

So...what do we do now?

Dunno.

Can we try it?

It's different now. There's Lester.

Can we try it anyway?

Don't think it's a good idea.

I've been wanting to kiss you ever since the first time we wrestled. Out in the leaves. All those times I stopped the fighting, the playing. It's b/c I was afraid I'd

Yellow Legal Pad Picked Up Off Floor Beside Jake's Bed 10:50 p.m.

I can't do this.

I'm sorry. I'm making you cheat.

No. It's more than that. This just feels so forced.

What do you mean?

Yr not sposed to plan out kissing someone. It's sposed to be spontaneous. Like yr just overcome w/ emotion & it leads → a kiss. You know you want to do it & it happens.

Maybe next time it'll be that way.

*I'm sorry, Jake. It doesn't feel right. Not sure there *should* be a next time.*

See? This is why I never tried anything.

I KNEW this would happen.

What would?

You wouldn't like me like that.

I do though. A whole lot.

Then why no next time?

For one thing, I'm dating someone. Who I like.

And aren't you afraid of ruining yr friendship w/ him too? Like w/ us?

It's different. It's not like he & I built up this big friendship before we started dating. Something I'd want to hold on to forever. I feel like I can experiment w/ him in a way that I can't w/ you.

Page Ripped from Yellow Legal Pad and Turned Over 11:08 p.m.

What abt how he's jealous of me? Doesn't that annoy you?

It's actually refreshing. I don't have to wonder what he's thinking. I know he'll always tell me. Even if he knows I won't like what he has to say.

I can be like that too.

**Can* you? You sure haven't been w/ me.*

Fine, so I'm no good @ confrontations. But. I think most ppl aren't good @ that. It's like yr trying to tell someone yr feelings in some rational way. But feelings ≠ rational. Like:

1 + 2 = sad
or
my fist + your arm = a bruise
= the only safe way I knew of getting physically close to you

+ the licking + punching + tickling + lifting upside down + throwing of pudding

Right.

Yr 1 weird dude.

You did it just as much as I did.

**Almost* as much.*

What a match we'd make.

Yeah. Then you could strike us on flint & start a mean-ass fire.

You realize yr never gonna be able to stop that, right?

But it also means no more boring conversations / news / ppl talking @ parties or bars.

New Page on Yellow Legal Pad 11:26 p.m.

Shit. I feel like I messed up big. In ways I'll never forgive myself for.

You've made things difficult for yrself. But don't you think you'll be different next time you like someone?

Who knows if there WILL be another person?

There's no other Xandra.

There'll be another person w/ a diff name.

Who I'd have to start ALL OVER with. Getting to know her / the nervousness. No thanks.

Why do you feel that way re: confrontations?

Told you why.

*Yeah, but not *everyone* feels that way. You make it sound like it's universal human behavior.*

Just b/c Lester = Mr. Communication doesn't mean most ppl are like him either.

Okay, so maybe he's the opposite extreme. But yr still an extreme.

I don't know. There's this letter I got from my mom after she visited. I've been thinking, maybe it explains how I am.

What'd it say?

Basically, how she never loved my dad.

She shouldn't've told you that.

I pretty much knew it anyway. Just wish I didn't have it in writing.

Why think she told you?

Wanted me to understand why she left my dad.

& do you?

Maybe a little. But there's so much about it that scares me. I mean, she left him b/c he's in his own world. Which is kinda like me, right?

But you have friends.

New Page on Yellow Legal Pad 11:38 p.m.

Sure, but I'm a weirdo. I write notes instead of talking. When there's nothing wrong w/ my voice.

True. So yr worried that yr like yr dad? & the same thing might happen to you?

That's part of it, I guess. Then there's my mom cheating. Which also reminds me of myself. Not that I've cheated. Never had a real girlfriend. But what I've done = just as bad.

So yr like both of them?

Both of their worst traits.

But the biggest thing that's bothering me is:

if . . .

Mom + Dad = Jake

and . . .

Mom + Dad = no love

then . . .

Jake = product of no love

Can't think like that. They had you & here you are. Even if they weren't madly in love, they liked each other enuf to get married & have you . . . & they love you now, even if they show it in funny ways.

My mom married my dad b/c that's what ppl did after dating a long time. Then they had me b/c yr supposed to have kids when you get married. I'm just a step in a chain of events that was "supposed to" happen. The WAY things are done.

*...& how do *you* think things should be done?*

I think you should really really be sure you love someone + that they love you back before you get into a relationship.

But how do you know you love them until you get into the relationship?

Yr friends 1st. Then you get so close that you fall in love.

But what if you get so close that you don't ever want to lose them & yr afraid that a relationship might change the friendship so much that it dies?

I guess that's possible. But what if you become even closer + you love each other so much that it lasts forever? Isn't that a possibility too?

*That's a really romantic way of looking at it. But in order for that to happen, I think you need to be honest from the start re: how you feel. Risk rejection so you *can* become that close w/ the person.*

I always thought that telling you what I wanted would keep me from getting it . . . b/c you wouldn't want the same thing + it would drive you away from me. But yr saying that's not true.

I'm saying I guess we'll never know. It could've gone either way.

That Page Ripped Out of Pad and Turned Over 11:53 p.m.

How're you doing w/ all of this talking abt emotions?

Not exactly enjoying it. But there's something nice abt it. I'm just glad we don't do it more often. We'd use up too much paper!

Well, I'm glad we got this all out. I understand things a little more.

We done?

I think that's it for me. Except for one thing. Now that everything's out in the open, can I read that letter you wrote to me?

That + all the others?

There's more than 1?

Lots.

Let me read them?

I would. Except you can't.

Getting cryptic on me again?

No. Really. It's impossible. They're gone.

Threw them away?

Burned em. On the beach. Or tried to at least. But the sand was too wet + they wouldn't really catch fire. Not like my jacket sleeve, which apparently = pretty flammable. Anyway, the letters are somewhere in the lake now.

Too bad. I bet they were good.

Cardboard Backing of Yellow Legal Pad 12:02 a.m.

Okay...so...you sure there's nothing else on yr mind?

Yeah. I've had enough for today. Anyway, we're out of paper.

Easy to find more.

No thanks.

We good, then?

We're good.

Do I get a hug?

*That's *all*?*

More like it.

■ ■ ■

Black-and-White-Speckled English Composition Notebook 1:07 a.m.

Steven,

This whole not talking thing was supposed to get me out of trouble. And maybe it has. In certain ways. Like how I have a good excuse to not talk to my ex best friend Sean when I see him. Which isn't much at all. That's something I used to feel really bad about. And I still do. But not as much. Because. I don't think we'd have much to talk about anyway. We're into different stuff now.

But the thing is:

not saying anything =
just as much trouble as saying the WRONG thing
because . . .
keeping quiet about how you want kisses = no kisses
but . . .
writing notes = no help either
because . . .
pleading with someone to kiss you through notes also =
no kisses

Is everything in life like this? A series of losses? Even when you try to do something to fix what you've done wrong? You find that your solution messes up some other aspect of your life?

It's just, I can't think of any WORDS that could fix this.

—Jake

By the time it's light out, dime-size flakes are drifting to the ground.

Dry-Erase Board on Jake's Door 7:15 a.m.

Came to see if you want to join me for bfast. Yr probly already there...

■ ■ ■

Dry-Erase Board on Jake's Door 8:02 a.m.

Must've missed you. How bout lunch? 12:30 in student center lobby.

■ ■ ■

Butcher Paper Beside Stolen Sign Collection on Roger's Wall 4:01 p.m.

What do you MEAN, What's UP with me?

Just because I'm not constantly smiling doesn't mean something's WRONG.

Maybe I'm just tired from finals.

You guys done soon?

Yeah. Just got to turn in my English journal + finish a paper over break.

How do you want to celebrate?

Come write with me. It's depressing being the only one. I've gotten used to you doing it too.

The other day that cute chick with the glasses asked what was up with the big roll of paper in your room. She walks by here all the time.

I've got an urge to steal something. Maybe a mailbox.

How?

Have to think about it.

I have an idea. How about we get layed?

Again . . . I ask . . . how?

Pitchfuck.

Which has never worked for you in the past.

Its always worth a try. Girls go there wanting to hook up.

True.

I *just* can't wait till I'm back in my own room. Have some private time with my own trusty hand. You're so lucky Jake. Room to yourself.

Who needs there own room?

You do it in here?

Only when your not around. Or asleep.

That is *wrong!* ~~What do you~~ How do you clean up?

Socks.

I am never touching your socks again!

What do you use? Huh, Mr. Sanitery? Sanitery napkins?

I do it in the *shower* here. But when I'm home I use *tissues* or toilet paper.

Lets ask Mr. Experience. What do you use when your with a woman?

Whatever's around. Sock, t.p., underwear, shirt.

See?

Nastiness!

It all washes out.

& girls don't care when you use your clothes?

Nope.

I will never understand the female species. They want you to bring them flowers, be clean shaven, but it's fine with them if you mop up with your shirt?

Maybe you should ask glasses girl to weigh in on this when she passes by.

■ ■ ■

Dry-Erase Board on Jake's Door 5:32 p.m.

Dinner? Come get me. Whenever.

Dry-Erase Board on Jake's Door 6:33 p.m.

Got hungry. I'll be in the corner by the windows.

Dry-Erase Board on Jake's Door 7:18 p.m.

Back in my room now. Find me later?

■ ■ ■

Pocket-Size Graph-Paper Notepad with Orange Cover 7:52 p.m.

1 please.
Thanks.

Torn Corner of Graph Paper Slid Over Concession Stand Counter 7:56 p.m.

sm popcorn + lg coke, pls

Back of Ripped Movie Ticket Handed to Cashier 7:58 p.m.

Thanks!

■ ■ ■

From: aflash@citycollege.edu
To: jjacobsen@citycollege.edu
Sent: Today 11:04 p.m.
Subject: are we still friends?

i feel like you're avoiding me. are you? i thought we were cool.

i've been cleaning out my backpack. keep finding napkins with our notes on them.

~x~

■ ■ ■

Black-and-White-Speckled English Composition Notebook 12:02 a.m.

Steven,

Have you ever gotten so sad that it actually feels GOOD to do something you know will make you even sadder? Maybe that sounds totally strange. But it's what I did tonight.

I went to this movie, *The Man Who Laughs.* At that old theater with the stage + built-in organ. They had a real live mini orchestra behind the screen. And once in a while the projector guy would mess with the lighting so you could see the musicians in the middle of the movie. Which added to the weirdness + spookiness of it all. I'm not someone who normally cries at movies. But tonight . . . I cried through the entire thing. I mean, I'd stop sometimes. But then I'd remember that in one of these red fuzzy seats, this girl I'm crazy about was HOLDING HANDS with some other guy. Under those little lights on the ceiling that're supposed to look like stars. I couldn't stop thinking that THIS was the place where things had built up between them so much that they came home and screwed.

Plus, there was the whole love story in the movie. Which really was pretty cheesy. With the blind girl all into the guy who's got a freaky permanent smile. I won't ruin it in case you haven't seen it. It's just, this is the sort of thing I would usually find SO annoying. But for some reason the tears kept coming. What sentimental bullshit.

Excuse my language,

Jake

The following afternoon. Under a sky that hasn't been blue for weeks.

Dry-Erase Board on Jake's Door 2:06 p.m.

Where were you last night? Should've come to Ψ. Lots of dancing babes.

■ ■ ■

From: jjacobsen@citycollege.edu
To: aflash@citycollege.edu
Sent: Today 3:35 p.m.
Subject: I hate to do this via email...

...but I'd feel terrible doing this in person. The thing is. I HAVE been avoiding you. You're right. We were cool. We are cool. But I just. Can't. Get. Over. You. Kissing. Someone. Else. Now that I know it could've been me.

Where this leaves us, I'm not sure. But I know I need to be away from you for a while. That's not to say I won't be there when and if it ends with you know who.

I can't believe that of all those letters I could've sent you, blabbing about us, this is the one I'm actually sending you. I wish I could be giving you something you'd like more. But I guess that's what I get for waiting.

J

■ ■ ■

From: aflash@citycollege.edu
To: jjacobsen@citycollege.edu
Sent: Today 4:51 p.m.
Subject: suckiness

j,

this is totally your call, so you should do whatever you need to do. but please know that it's not at all what i want. and i'm not going to let you go easily. i feel like there's still so much we haven't done. like swim in the lake in the summer. remember how we wanted to do it again... when it was warm enough? and i still owe you a *major* tooth-brushing... in return for that extra-special face-brushing you gave me. anyway, i'll respect your need for distance. but don't consider me gone. i'm still just down the hall.

i'm leaving early tomorrow morning. so i guess if i don't see you tonight, i won't see you till after the new year. Well... enjoy your break. i hope it's on a small part of your body... like a finger or toe... so it doesn't hurt too much.

~x~

■ ■ ■

Dry-Erase Board on Jake's Door 6:07 p.m.

Are you hiding in there? Come out tonight.

■ ■ ■

From: jjacobsen@citycollege.edu
To: aflash@citycollege.edu
Sent: Today 8:12 p.m.
Subject: RE: suckiness

I wish there was something I could do to SHOW you how much I hope we swim in the lake this summer. That's a long way off. We'll have to see.

> enjoy your break. i hope it's on a small part of your body... like a finger or toe... so it doesn't hurt too much.
It IS on a small part of my body. Only it hurts A LOT. Somewhere in the left side of my chest.

J

■ ■ ■

Dry-Erase Board on Roger and Paul's Door 9:19 p.m.

Sorry—just felt like being alone.

I'll go with you tonight. But not to ψ. I'm afraid I'll get beat up by some drunk bros.

Any other party. I could use a distraction.

■ ■ ■

Pocket-Size Graph-Paper Notepad with Orange Cover 11:03 p.m.

I'm gonna sit over there for a while. Dancing makes me so hot.

Thanks, yes, I know I've always been SO HOT.
Now I'm even hotter.

Pocket-Size Graph-Paper Notepad with Orange Cover 11:10 p.m.

Girl in all black: Last family vacation was in Florida when she was 10. She picked up a lizard by its tail and the body dropped off and ran away.

Guy w/ swishy bangs: Lost the D of his magnetic letters under the fridge, so could never use them to spell his name.

Girl standing against wall by keg: Was the last of her friends to need a bra. And so never realized that she had the nicest hair + eyes + butt of the whole pack.

Hey, I want in on this! I see the girls watching you. Your even a magnet when you write to yourself!

They're not watching.

<u>Are</u> watching! At least that cutie walking over there was. See?

Who?

Oh no. I was writing about her. She must've seen me checking her out.

Damn, so I don't have a chance. I'm outa here.

Pocket-Size Graph-Paper Notepad with Orange Cover 11:32 p.m.

Hi.

Yeah. I'm not talking. Stopped over a month ago.

Not really sure anymore. It made sense at the time. Now it just seems like I can't start again until I think of something good to say. I've become this "guy who doesn't talk." If I do talk it'll feel like a big deal.

Sure, have a seat. I don't think he's coming back.

Yeah, it's loud. Speakers are right there. Here, you can use this if you want.

Thanks, this is better. I feel like I'm always yelling at parties.

Don't like parties?

They're fine. But I'd rather really get to know 1 or 2 people than get lost in the crowd.

Know what you mean.

You drawing or something? Looked like you were concentrating really hard.

Just guessing things about people.

Can I see?

It's not really that interesting.

Can I see anyway?

~~No, I don't think you'd~~ What the hell. Sure. Have a look.

Pocket-Size Graph-Paper Notepad with Orange Cover 11:40 p.m.

Girl in all black: Last family vacation was in Florida when she was 10. She picked up a lizard by its tail and the body dropped off and ran away.

Guy w/ swishy bangs: Lost the D of his magnetic letters under the fridge, so could never use them to spell his name.

Girl standing against wall by keg: Was the last of her friends to need a bra. And so never realized that she had the nicest hair + eyes + butt of the whole pack.

That's me?

Back of That Page 11:41 p.m.

That's why I didn't want you to see.

No, it's flattering. And partly true. I was a late bloomer.

The rest is true too.

You think?

Definitely. I was only GUESSING about your eyes from far away. But they're the coolest green I've ever seen. With those little flecks of brown . . . wow! And your hair looks . . . well, like it'd be fun to touch. So brown it's black. And the ringlets. You could stick your finger right inside. And . . . um . . . I won't get into the other part. Let's just say I like it. This is embarrassing. You must feel weird.

Having a cute guy tell me how attractive he thinks I am?

I don't seem creepy?

No.

Freaky?

Charming.

For real?

For real.

You really think I'm cute?

Sure.

But I'm all gangly.

I'm into awkward boys.

Hey. Is it OK if I'm honest about something?

You've been lying so far?

No. It's just. I'm not good at stuff like this.

Stuff like this?

I don't know. Whatever's happening right now. I'm no good at it.

You seem fine to me. Nervous, maybe. But so am I.

I don't want to be presumptuous.

I have a feeling you won't be.

I'm just in a pretty crappy mood tonight. So don't take this personally—but I don't really feel like talking / writing about anything. Just wanna watch people. It's not that I'm not into you. Ugh, I'm digging myself into a bottomless pit.

No. I like watching too. OK if I stay? I won't bother you.

Sure.

Pocket-Size Graph-Paper Notepad with Orange Cover 12:19 a.m.

Hey... see that girl over there? The one who doesn't move her arms while dancing. What do you think she wishes she'd never thrown out?

Her Hello Kitty backpack. It'd be so hip now!

Good one! Your turn.

OK, the guy who's jumping up and down. What's he hiding from his mom?

How much she's disappointed him. But he's thinking maybe in a couple weeks, he'll finally admit it to her. Even if it means a terribly a.w.k.w.a.r.d. confrontation.

Before sunrise in mid-December, the air biting at bare fingertips.

Pocket-Size Graph-Paper Notepad with Orange Cover 5:05 a.m.

½ lb. of gouda please

In a chunk.

That's all.

Thanks!

Pocket-Size Graph-Paper Notepad with Orange Cover 5:11 a.m.

Don't need a bag.

Yeah, I've got laryngitis.

■ ■ ■

Dry-Erase Board on Xandra's Door 5:29 a.m.

I know it's too late, but . . .

↓

Permanent Marker on Red Wax Covering Hunk of Gouda Outside Xandra's Door 5:31 a.m.

something I shoulda
given you a
long time
ago

■ ■ ■

Black-and-White-Speckled English Composition Notebook 6:15 a.m.

Steven,

This is my last entry before turning in my nonjournal. And there's a lot to tell you. The MAJOR thing is, I said my 1st words today. They were: Get. Off. Yeah, I know, haha. Luckily, the guy I said it to didn't follow my instructions. Anyway. I haven't said anything else. But maybe that's just cause everyone I know is either asleep or has already left for break.

Here's what happened. Well. It's a long story. But basically, I needed to get some cheese for a friend. Yes. At 5:00 in the morning. As you can imagine, I was pretty sleepy. I wasn't really paying attention to where I was walking. And so when I was in line to pay, I got too close to this ginormous man in front of me. With cinder blocks for feet. He took a step backwards . . . and there you have it. GET OFF! I didn't even think about whether or not to say something. I just did it. Actually, I think that's the best way to have it happen. I'll write more about this in my "hows and whys" paper. Which I'm actually kinda looking forward to. Also scared. But in a waiting-for-the-roller-coaster way.

Then there's this other thing I want to tell you about. This girl I bought the cheese for. She's way into this Batman guy. Listed himself under that name in the phone book. I was all jealous (I guess I still am) because when I was a kid I always dressed up as Batman. Which he NEVER did. And so I felt like this Batman character was stealing my act. But you know? I think if I could be ANY superhero, I wouldn't do generic saving like Batman. This might sound weird, but I'd be Potential Energy Man. What I'd do is pump the potential back into things. Into people. I'd make it so you could start over at the top of the hill. And sure, your energy would turn "kinetic" as you rolled down. But then I'd be waiting at the bottom and I'd have my Potential Pump and you'd be able to start over again. At the top. Full of potential. And this time you'd know better. You'd use it well.

That might all sound depressing. Because there's no such thing as a Potential Pump. And what's gone is gone. Like this cheese girl. It's killing me that I can't have her. Or that I COULD'VE had her and I can't get that chance back. But you know? I went with my friends to a party last night. Which I haven't done in a long-ass time. Because I thought parties were stupid + boring. And they can be. But there's also something fun about being around people getting silly. Trying to figure out what's REALLY going on in their lives. And watching your friends' pickup lines flop . . . yet again. There's also something liberating about letting a flirty girl know you're attracted to her. But to put off hooking up. Not cause you're holding out for someone else. Or because you think she's ditzy. But because you're just not in the mood.

Don't worry, though. I'll be back on top soon enough.

Literally,

Jake

Thank you thank you thank you to...

Jamie Fink for giving me a science lesson while driving.

Josh Frank and Jeff Kliegman for getting bored
in a RE-COCK-ULOUSLY long line.

Naomi Kraut for filling a little red spiral-bound notebook
with me on a winter afternoon.

Jonathan Menjivar for catching all the funny that I miss.

My editor, Eden Edwards,
for encouraging me to come up with new ideas.

And my parents for convincing me that working on those
ideas is worthwhile.

—H. F.